Jersey Diner

Jersey Diner

Say You're Only For Me

Lisa Diane Kastner

Running Wild Press

Visit Lisa on the web at www.lisadianekastner.com

Educators, librarians, book clubs (as well as the eternally curious), go to www.lisadianekastner.com for teaching tools.

ISBN 978-0-9977788-0-9 (pbk)

Library of Congress Control Number 2016914884

Printed in the United States of America.

For Poppi
You live in the hearts, minds, souls,
and thoughts of all those who loved you.
This number is innumerable.

Jonathan Pearce. Two words. Four syllables. What beautiful sounds they make. The sound of lovers calling. Of protection. Of hope. And he will be here. Soon.

Chapter 1

By 10 a.m. the Oaklyn Diner had emptied. Decades ago, Mr. Polyxena had bought the place as a wedding gift for his future missus. The retro jukeboxes remained silent. No bodies warmed the mauve plastic seat covers. Empty open traincaresque windows dominated the exterior walls and left the place feeling wide-eyed and exposed. After a spell of rain and fog, sunlight spilled into the space. In the absence of customers, I filled salt and pepper shakers and put them on a metallic tray. Blondie's "Call Me" played on the kitchen radio.

The diner was nearly quiet except for the radio's tinny sound. Mr. Polyxena, or Mr. P as he preferred to be called, read the morning *Courier Post* in his office while he sipped his fifth coffee. Mrs. Polyxena hummed an unnamed tune while she replenished stock. She came out of the back and wiped her hands on a stained dishtowel.

Her white blonde hair had been poofed to twice the size of her head. She wore one of her favorite jogging suits – bright green with a yellow stripe down the side. Her acrylic nails had been painted to match the stripe.

"Mrs. P, do you mind if I step out for a sec? I want to check on my dad," I said. He had acted odd this morning and I had been having trouble focusing ever since. I placed my emptied tray of salt and pepper shakers underneath the counter.

"You run home. Monica and I will watch your tables." Monica had just returned from a smoke break and nodded in agreement.

Mrs. P wandered to the back. Her tune resembled a 1920s song, one she had hummed many times before. The diner was a five-minute walk from my house, but if I sprinted I could make it in two. I hung up my apron and threw on my jacket. "Don' forget," Mrs. P said, "get back for afternoon rush."

The sidewalk had been splattered with puddles. I tried to hop over them, nearly soaked my tennis shoes, and ran down the street regardless. Straight across from the diner was a small one-way street and then a line of houses, some converted into local businesses, like Joe's Shoe Repair Shop and the Mystical Fortune Seer. Just beyond the strip of buildings was a four lane highway and beyond that a Wendy's and a McDonald's and a Kmart. All seemed to have popped up in the span of days. Previously emptied row homes and Section 8 housing had been demolished to accommodate the stores that also dominated my television screen.

I turned the corner and ran down my small street lined with ranchers. One after another had been built like someone took a set of Legos and plopped them next to each other. Some had been sided, others made of brick. Each one had been built with a one-car garage and gravel driveway. If I looked at them too long, I'd be claustrophobic.

I slipped the house key into the doorknob and shook the knob until I felt the click of the lock. The door swung open and released the stale air with a tinge of Pine-Sol. My parents had bought the 1950s two-bedroom rancher when they married. I don't think they updated a single thing.

I entered the living room to find the television vibrating with light. The sound turned to full volume. Jonathan Pearce told Meg Ryan he loved her as she leapt into his arms.

Even at his worst, my dad didn't leave the TV on.

"Dad? Are you still here?" When he didn't answer, I went to the kitchen. On the kitchen counter I found a box of opened corn flakes, a half-eaten banana, and a container of heavy cream. The percolator had been left on, the kitchen reeked of burnt coffee. I covered my mouth with a kitchen towel and pulled the plug on the coffee pot, not taking the chance of touching the pot and burning my fingers. I sniffed the heavy cream to make sure it hadn't gone bad and opened the fridge door that creaked with its own weight. I placed the creamer back on its proper shelf, carefully closing the refrigerator door.

I hoped he would come out of a room and welcome me home or come through the house's front door and announce he had gotten that job. The one that would return him to where he was before Mama got sick. I listened and waited.

From Dad's bedroom came a faint sound. The voice of Humphrey Bogart echoed through the hallway. It was the other television, the one in their bedroom. I walked to the room and pushed open the door. "Dad?"

I didn't want to enter. I didn't want to find out what went wrong. I wanted someone to yell, "Cut!" like in the movies and then Dad would run from behind door number three and tell me the last few years were a test. A test of the emergency broadcast system, but only a test.

The windows had been covered with heavy blankets. His room was virtually empty except for the television's flickering lights. I sat on his bed and placed my hand on his shoulder.

Humphrey warned Audrey Hepburn to stay away from his brother. *Sabrina* had been my parents' favorite movie. They had seen it on their first date. It was a movie my father had played over and over again in the last few weeks.

"Dad?" I whispered his name underneath the movie sounds. I don't know why I whispered. The words felt more intimate the closer I leaned into him. The images of Humphrey and Audrey pounced on the sparse items in the bedroom. Dresser drawers closed tightly. Each piece of clothing had been taken out and arranged on top in a neat row.

"Dad?" I repeated. I lightly shook him. He didn't respond. I felt myself brimming with emotion as my eyes filled with tears. A picture of my mama as a young woman remained prominent in the center of my parents' dresser. She played at the beach in her polka dot bathing suit under a big umbrella. She smiled at the person behind the camera. A warm smile, the kind that made me want to talk to her. My hands began to shake with the realization that he wasn't going to respond.

Compressed and stacked beer cans had been piled in the trash-can next to the dresser. He had left everything tidy, as she would have wanted. The mirror over their chest of drawers reflected us on the bed with him under the foam green comforter and me on top. Unable to look into my own eyes, I turned away.

"Dad, are you awake?" I whispered again. I put my hand before his mouth. The warmth of his breath heated my palm. I noted his chest rising and falling. Maybe I should have checked his breath sooner. Then I wouldn't feel like a surge of electrical energy had zapped through me. He turned over and let out a snore. "Dad, wake up." I squeezed his shoulder. The least he could have done was turn off the TV before he passed out. I had a wild enough imagination, I didn't need him helping me out.

Chapter 2

The day began with Rich coming in for lunch. We had gone to the same high school, except he graduated two years ago. All the girls dreamed about him. Me too, I guess. He played every sport. His dark blonde hair kissed his shoulders.

"Hey, Lauren. You still talk to that Jen girl?"

"You mean Julie?" Right after graduation ceremonies last week, Julie jumped in her boyfriend's cherry red Camaro convertible and took off.

"Yeah. Julie."

"No. Not really." As Julie drove away, she called, "*I'm getting the hell out of Jersey. You should too.*" I watched as she sped away, leaving me with a blank piece of paper tied in a red ribbon representing my diploma. My father hadn't made it to my graduation. His buddies' exploits in "interviewing," another word for going door-to-door to find dayworker jobs. In celebration or consolation, they then entered the nearest bars. I knew this because this had been his M.O. for years. I had hoped that maybe this one day he would have broken the habit.

Rich's words, "That's a shame," knocked me out of the memory. He took out a quarter and then inserted it into the nearest jukebox. Jon Bon Jovi's *Runaway* clicked through the speakers. Rich looked back down at the menu and placed his standard order. Before he graduated, he never spoke to me. In high school, I wasn't tall enough or pretty enough or popular enough. I don't think he even knew I existed. Non-athletic, short girls with mousy hair and round faces weren't popular. The tall, thin, cute-as-a-Barbie-doll girls were invited to parties and asked to the prom. Julie had been one of those girls, even though she read stories by Chekhov and never once turned down a good mystery, especially Sherlock Holmes.

I wrote down Rich's order and headed back to the kitchen, passing the metal chairs with red glitter plastic seats that lined the faux marble counter. More people danced in the fifties memorabilia on the walls than could be found populating the diner. Bored, Monica polished her fingernails in a corner booth. Mrs. P had sent the third waitress on duty, Dotty, home. "Not busy enough," Mrs. P had said. "Come back tonight. We should be busy then."

When I reached the kitchen, I found Mrs. P reading European gossip magazines. Her dayglow fingertips blurred with the swoosh of each page.

"Order up," I said and left the order slip on the breezeway connecting the kitchen to the dining area.

Mrs. P closed the magazine and picked up the grey-green paper. After looking at my scribble, she dropped two hamburger patties onto the grill. The smell of cooking meat and the sizzle of fat accompanied wafts of smoke that clouded above. I watched the swirls and puffs as an exhaust vent sucked them through.

My stomach turned with the thought of what waited for me at home. I had done my best to help my father since Mom passed away when I was in middle school. An unexpected illness. One that affected my father in ways I don't think any of us anticipated. Even Mr. and Mrs. P had tried to help him out but he refused, preferring the company and assistance of his crew.

The clinking of metal against metal brought me back to the room. Mr. P flipped the burgers with his favorite spatula causing a billow of smoke to escape the grill. As he pressed down on the patties, fat jumped from the meat and into the air. In the middle of the room, a wooden block doubled as a cutting board and table.

I leaned against the kitchen counter and looked into the main diner. Rich stared out of the window, waiting for his food. A young couple sat in a booth, the woman animated. A guy in a grey suit relaxed at the counter, fingering the *Philadelphia Inquirer*. A typical lunch hour. Across the highway was a Wendy's that had a string of cars waiting to place their orders. Even though the Ps hadn't talked to me about it, I wondered how much longer we could last with a handful of customers. Since I started working for them when I was sixteen, more fast food restaurants were built nearby and fewer customers came to our door.

"Can I look at those?" I pointed to the magazines on the kitchen counter. Normally, Mrs. P and I would look through them together. My favorite was *Hello!,* a British celebrity magazine. When she talked to me about movie stars, she reminded me of when I was little and mama gazed blankly at the shadows before her while I read. My mom smiled at the *Star's* descriptions. I loved to see my mama smile.

Mrs. P flipped the magazine closed and reached behind her to pick up the order from her husband. "Maybe later." She handed me Rich's order. As I turned to serve him, she motioned for me to come closer. She sat on a wooden stool next to the butcher block and glided her fingernails across the top. She felt the indentations where the knife had sunken into the wood. As I approached, I smelled her favorite perfume, Chanel No. 5. "Lauren. Why don't you ask Rich out? He's a good boy. He's a hard worker."

I almost laughed. "I don't think so. He'd never talk to me like that."

"You'd make a good couple. Just imagine the babies you could have. With your eyes and his hair. Oh! They'd be beautiful." Without looking at me, she teased. "You never know."

“I’ll think about it,” I said and exited the kitchen to serve Rich. Mrs. P didn’t understand. I knew who I was meant to be with.

“What’s up with Mrs. P?” Rich asked.

“Nothing. Why?”

“She keeps coming over here and winking at me. See, she’s doing it again.”

I looked over my shoulder to find Mrs. P in the breezeway. As soon as I turned she abruptly looked away and dusted the wall. Great. I absolutely loved her, even when she played matchmaker. “She’s just being herself. Here ya go.” I placed the plate before him. He smirked.

On my way back to the kitchen, I poured a cup of coffee. I had gotten in the habit of double checking on our bills and secretly paying the ones my father forgot about. I felt like there were too many bills to go through, too much work to be done at home and even more here. My dad did his best, but sometimes I felt overwhelmed.

I joined Mrs. P in the back and sat next to her. In my head I rehearsed what I wanted to say. I needed her help.

I fiddled with the magazines and flipped the pages with each thought. Just when I opened my mouth to ask, the bells above the front door jingled. I craned my neck to the doorway. A man walked in wearing a three-quarter length leather black coat. His slick brown hair hugged his head. Black wrap-around sunglasses covered his eyes. Behind him, three people, two men and a woman, followed. They dressed in shades of black. Each one behind the other like something from a dance show. The man in front glided his hand across the counter and the plastic seats. His fingertips squeaked from the moisture of his skin rubbing against the unrelenting surface. He walked up and down the aisle as the rest of the group trailed after him. “We can do a lot with this place,” the man said.

"Michael, we can do the scene where Alexander and Jannit have their first big dinner together. Over here," the woman responded.

I hoped Mrs. P would help them, but instead she cleaned the grill.

"May I help you?" I stuck my head through the double doors. The sound of the doors opening broke their conversation.

Michael, the leader of the group, resumed talking to his friends. "Right, right. And what about when she—" he looked around the room and tapped his fingers to his chin. "You know. You think that can work?"

"Excuse me? May I help you?" I repeated.

"Hold on," said the woman. "It's Jonathan. He wants to know if we've found the location." She held the phone next to her chest.

Michael hesitated for a moment. He looked around the diner, touched the photos on the walls, tapped the counter and then sat on a stool.

"Tell him yes and he made a good choice. We'll call him in a few." The woman mumbled into her phone and shut it off as he stepped closer to me. He smelled of stale tobacco and day old clothes. He looked me up and down, assessing me. "May I speak to the manager?"

I touched my hand to my hair and wondered if my ponytail had come out of the rubber band. Mrs. P stuck her head through the breezeway and patted the counter, then she motioned to the back office. The three visitors exchanged glances.

"Mr. Polyxena's the manager. He's in the back. I'll get him for you," I said.

"Perfect."

I approached the tiny cubby-like room that housed Mr. P's office. In his small space he had a chair, a desk, the daily newspaper, and a small television with headphones.

I knocked on the doorframe. "There are some folks here to see you." Mr. P, a man with brown hair peppered with silver, got up from his chair. At five foot six, he stood an inch or two above me. Most days he could hide in his office without anyone bothering him. The leader's voice projected over my shoulder.

"Are you the manager?"

From the corner of my eye I saw Rich leave. He waved goodbye.

"I'm George Polyxena. And you are?" He extended his hand and the guy in the coat placed a card into his palm.

"I'm Michael Smarthey with Philadelphia Casting." I tried to read it as Mr. P looked over the card. "We're here to film a movie."

"It's starring Jonathan Pearce," the woman said.

"What did you say?" I asked.

"I said it's starring Jonathan Pearce."

"Not interested," Mr. P said. I turned to see Mrs. P approach. She nodded at me as if to say, "*Don' worry*."

"Hold on." Mrs. P stood next to her husband and placed her hand on the small of his back. "Isn't he the one in all of those—"

"Movies," said Michael Smarthey. "Yeah. He's one of them."

"Mrs. P?" I said.

"Alexandra, what." Mr. P said. She whispered in his ear. Mr. P was the practical one.

"We need a diner, just like this one," Mr. Smarthey said. Mr. and Mrs. P whispered to one another. Mr. Smarthey shifted his feet and looked at his cohorts. Mr. and Mrs. P continued their conversation. Mrs. P's motions more animated than her husband's. Mr. Smarthey cleared his throat. "And we'll pay. $14,000."

Mr. Polyxena's eyes widened as he looked over Mr. Smarthey's shoulder. "I'm not interested," he restated.

Behind Michael Smarthey, one of his assistants held a paper-wrapped burger with a yellow arch and a red M stamped across it. He chomped and swallowed the food in three bites and then crumpled the grease covered waste paper in the palm of his hand and tossed it onto the counter.

I started, "Mr. P. Are you sure about that because—"

"It's going to be a national—" Mr. Smarthey began.

"Not only am I not interested, but you're leaving." Mr. P returned the card and led them to the front door.

Mr. Smarthey's face contorted. His hand movement matched his words. "I don't understand. This is a—"

"No one comes into my place and disrespects it. No one." Mr. P picked up the remains from the counter and held it in front of Mr. Smarthey's face. I backed away from them.

"What—"

"Your assistant." I pointed at the male who followed Mr. Smarthey.

The assistant shrugged. "What?"

Mr. P stormed up to the man and grabbed his hand. "This. This is disrespect." He shoved the wrapping into the man's palm and Mr. P forced the guy's fingers around it, then met the man's gaze. Mr. P looked like he could have picked up the assistant and tossed him through the window.

"Get. Out."

The assistant shot a look at each of us. He must have been looking for someone to help him. Agape, the woman picked up the phone, ready to dial. Everything happened so quickly, I wasn't sure what to do.

"I'm sorry," the man said.

"Darleeng." Mrs. P paused next to her husband. "I don' think he means anything." Her hand traveled up his back and hovered at his shoulder.

"I don't care what he meant. You want a place, go to that junk across the street. No one—"

"Listen to the man in charge. This one's not so bright." Her lips close to his ear, she purred this just loud enough so we could hear it.

The guy winced at the comment.

"He started today." Mr. Smarthey said. "I'll reprimand him."

"Not good enough." Mr. P continued to stare down the assistant. The man crumbled like the wrapping.

"Joe, I need you to go outside." Mr. Smarthey stated.

As quickly as he had devoured the sandwich, Joe exited the diner.

"I apologize on his behalf. He won't be accompanying us to locations anymore." Mr. Smarthey said as the door whooshed closed.

"That was insensitive and inappropriate. Your place of business is one of a kind. It needs to be captured on film," said the lady.

Joe sat on the hood of the midnight blue Cavalier rental car. Mr. P approached the freshly cleaned glass window. "They take my business."

"I'm sorry?" the woman said. Across the highway the Wendy's remained alive with activity.

"I said, they take my business." He pointed to the fast food chain. "Before they came. Now . . ." Mr. P motioned throughout the empty diner, his arm taut with the thought. Mrs. P placed her hand onto his shoulder and rubbed his back.

"This is fine. We're always fine," she whispered to him. His muscles released with her touch.

"Double." Mr. Smarthey blocked Mr. P's view of Joe.

Mr. P shifted away from Mrs. P and stood tall. "Double?"

Mrs. P mouthed to me, "*Don' worry.*"

"Let me think." Mr. P returned to his office. Mrs. P followed. The door clicked shut. It must have been really close in there.

The female assistant asked, "Are they coming back?"

"I think so," I said. "Do you want some lunch? We have specials. The most popular item on the menu is a cheeseburger platter." I wasn't sure what else to say but as long as they were here . . .

Mr. Smarthey watched the office door, the Ps behind it, no sign of their return. He looked at his watch and then at his assistant.

"How important?" he asked her.

She lifted her cell phone. "He sounded adamant."

"Who sounded adamant?" I asked.

They exchanged a look and Mr. Smarthey pulled up a chair. He motioned her to do the same.

"The platter sounds fine," he said.

I went to the kitchen and imitated what Mrs. P had done a thousand times. I wanted to yell behind Mr. P and tell Mr. Smarthey that we wanted them to film here. In the diner Mr. Smarthey and his assistant whispered to each other. He picked up her phone and talked. I hurried to retrieve the fries from the fryer, careful not to get burned from the splattering oil. The air, thick with grease, coated my skin and filled my nostrils. Maybe if I give the movie people an extra helping of fries then they'll calm down.

I grabbed a couple of Cokes and placed the platters before them. "Here ya go. Anything else I can get for you?"

"Just ketchup," the woman said as she picked up a fry and blew on it before she munched on its end. They silently ate their burgers. I had never seen anyone eat so carefully. It was more like they picked at the food. Reminded me of little kids trying to make the plates look like they had eaten a lot. I stayed behind the counter and found things to do. The front door chimed with a customer. Mr. Lettice, a regular, sat at his favorite counter spot and nodded. I smiled back and greeted him but I never took my eyes away from the office door. Neither could Mr. Smarthey.

I served Mr. Lettice who seemed oblivious to the newbies. "Where's Mrs. P?" He asked after he had placed his order for his typical BLT sandwich with extra mayonnaise.

"She's kind of busy right now," I said. "She'll be back in a few."

A couple of other customers came in and placed orders. I ran between the kitchen and the tables with the biggest broadest smile. I checked on Mr. Smarthey and his assistant to be sure they had what they needed. What felt like hours passed before the Ps came out of the office and joined me behind the counter.

"What's that smell? Burgers?" Mr. P asked.

"They're having lunch," I said.

"See." Mrs. P nudged her husband.

Mr. Smarthey swallowed a bite of his burger. He had just taken a real bite of his sandwich when the Ps came out. Mr. Smarthey chewed and chewed then gulped his Coke. He wiped his mouth and continued to chew and raised his hand, silently asking us to wait.

"Fine. You finish, then we'll talk. Lauren. Come get me when they're done. You know where I'll be." In two steps he returned to his office and sealed the door. Mrs. P went over to Mr. Lettice and greeted her old friend.

Only hours before I had wondered if my life could go back to how it had been when I was little and I only worried about finger painting and not getting ketchup on my white t-shirt. Minutes ago, I handed a movie scout a bottle of ketchup and prayed that Mr. P wouldn't ruin the one chance I have to meet Jonathan.

Mr. Smarthey ate so quickly I almost got sick. Fat from the burger slid down his chin as he swallowed. He grabbed a napkin and wiped his face. "All right." He took a deep breath. "The things I do," he said to the plate splattered with crumbs. His assistant gave him an uncomfortable smile.

For the first time the man looked me in the eyes like an actual person, then waited for me to motion him to follow. Like he should have from the get go. I knocked on the office door. It opened with only the sound of a turning lock. Mr. Smarthey entered and shut it behind him. He moved so fast I couldn't get inside. I thumped the door to no answer, and then returned to refill Mr. Lettice's glass. The hubbub of customers nearly gone. Mr. Lettice took the final bite from his BLT and wiped his mouth.

"Are they serious?" He motioned in the direction of the assistant.

"I guess so," I said.

Mrs. P came from behind the counter and said, "We'll see." She went into the office and closed the door. Now it must have been really tight in there. Even with that thought, I wished I was inside.

"This would be good, yeah?" Mr. Lettice asked.

"This would be good," I said.

Mrs. P eased out of the office minutes afterward. "Don' worry," she whispered to me and patted my hand.

The cars still lined up at the fast food restaurants across the street. The lines never seemed to end. Mr. Smarthey's assistant shuffled a folder full of papers. Read one, scribbled a few words, flipped it over and then did the same. Over and over again. She checked her watch.

"Can I get you a refill of soda?" I asked her.

She looked at her watch again, then out the window where Joe leaned against their rental car, then at the office.

"Sure. Why not?"

I poured her another glass with lots of ice. By the time I reached the table, streams of perspiration had covered the cup. When I removed my hand, my fingerprints remained in the dew.

Mrs. P eased back into the office. I tried to look busy. I didn't want to seem like I was anxious to find out what went on. The female assistant talked on her phone. Every once in a while she looked at the office door and then lowered her voice.

Mr. Lettice paid his check and left along with the other sparse customers. A tall guy with a windbreaker came in, used the bathroom and bought a candy bar from the main counter. The mailman dropped off a stack for the Ps. A young couple came in and ordered two specials. I served them like I normally would. I had the hardest time focusing though. I couldn't tell you what anyone looked like or what they had ordered. They were simply unwanted distractions.

I refilled the sugar bowls, careful not to spill any on the counter. Checked the time. Wiped down the counters again. Wiped down the tables. Looked at the clock. What took them so long? I tried to think of a reason to knock on the door.

The front door swung open. "What's going on?" Joe stuck his head inside.

"It'll be awhile," the female assistant said.

"I didn't mean to—"

"Joe. Don't worry about it. He's taking care of it. Go back outside," she said. He zipped up his coat and then ducked out and slid back to his spot on the car.

"Do you need anything?" I asked her. I tried to think of something to talk to her about. Something we might have in common. Maybe chat about Jonathan.

"I'm fine," she said.

"Do you always do this?" I sat in the chair across from her. I crossed my hands in front of me, then put them on my lap, then put them in my pockets. My hands felt oversized so I put them at my sides.

"Do what?" She covered the mouthpiece of her phone.

"I wondered if you always check out locations other than movie sets. I mean you can do anything in a movie set."

She spoke into the phone. "Give me a sec." Then she returned to me. "Sometimes we'd rather be on location. It has more character. It's more interesting for the audience instead of a made up place or a reproduction. Authenticity counts." She said this like anyone and everyone knew it.

With her response, I forgot what else I wanted to say. Her words made the differences between us even clearer.

"Interesting." I thanked her and cleared the table. I couldn't think of anything else to talk about. I had interrupted her conversation and if I did it one more time then she would be angry. After I had cleaned the tables for the thirtieth or seventieth time, the office door opened.

"We'll provide a contract. That's standard." Mr. Smarthey straightened the line of his jacket.

"Fine. Fine," Mr. P said. They shook hands. Mrs. P left the office.

With a nod from Mr. Smarthey, the woman with the cell phone dialed and turned away from us. She whispered, "Jonathan? It's done."

Through the phone came a droning, the static, nondescript sound of someone too far away to be heard. She hung up the phone and nodded to Michael.

"Did you say he was here?" I asked.

"I'm sorry? Did I say who was here?"

"Jonathan."

She placed the phone in her bag and choked on a laugh. "Let's say he was tipped off that this might be a good spot."

"My secretary will be in touch. The diner must be closed during filming." Mr. Smarthey said.

No one had mentioned closing the diner. We couldn't do that. For a second I thought Mr. P looked frightened. I don't think the Ps had closed the diner in the years I'd worked for them, not even for Christmas and New Year's. Smarthey's statement made this feel like an ending, but the end of what I didn't know. Mr. Smarthey shook Mr. and Mrs. P's hands and then the movie people flew out of the front door as if they had never walked in. I tried to digest what had happened. I replayed the conversation over and over. I wanted to find something to hold onto; still not sure I had witnessed what I thought I did.

I spent most of the night scrubbing the diner. The odor of Ajax and the gritty feeling of the cleanser comforted me. I felt accomplished as the sand of the cleanser crusted under my fingernails. Grounded me. The motion of cleaning was something I could count on to remain the same.

That evening we had two customers. One was Ms. Thompson who lived three blocks down the street. The other customer wandered into the diner, asked for the bathroom, and then bought a tuna melt with fries to go. When I rang him up, he kept his head down and handed me the money, grabbed the sandwich bag on his way out of the door. "Have a great day," I called after him.

During the downtime, I read my fan magazines in the back booth while Dotty studied for her exams at Camden County Community College. The streaming of car lights illuminated the streets. I felt the smudges break against the night. I let my mind wander into the magazine's photos. They took me to Hollywood, New York, San Francisco and London. I envisioned climbing into Jonathan's glistening red convertible, blacktop down, the wind blowing through my hair. He reached over and held my hand. The sun greeted us as we drove into it. I blushed with the thought. He said, *Lauren, I want to spend every moment with you.* The image floated through my head in to a meaningless jumble.

We closed the diner around 7:30. Even though our neon sign shone onto the turnpike, the chain eateries beaconed from across the highway.

Mr. P glared at the fast food restaurants. Cars pulled up into each competitor's drive-thru and sped off. He shook his fist and cursed. When Mr. P yelled at the Wendy's, I was safe. His voice filled the restaurant as he aimed anger at the cars. His protection of the diner and everything in it clearer with each word he spat.

Once he finished he stood stock-still, filled his lungs, held the air for one second and then sighed. His head dropped, body hunched over, arms loosely at his sides. The moment he released that last bit of anger, I absorbed it. The tension tightened my muscles, brought forward the angst and tiredness of the previous weeks.

Mrs. P seemed jittery since Mr. Smarthey and his entourage had visited. I couldn't tell if she was happy or not. She flipped through page after page of magazines and read articles about Jonathan and called me over. She said we needed to be prepared for the movie. Needed to know as much as we could about its stars. I scoffed. I knew more about all the stars than she'd ever know. "Okay, smartie," Mrs. P said. "What's his real name?"

"Jonathan Earl Percefino," I said.

"Where's he live?"

"He has homes in San Paulo, Brazil; Venice, Italy; Philadelphia, Pennsylvania; and Maui, Hawaii. His real home is in the suburbs of Los Angeles, California."

Her questions continued. In between the talks and my cleaning, Mr. P appeared and solemnly crouched in a booth. His actions reminded me of what waited at home.

I pushed a mop across the black and white linoleum floor, my arms sore from scrubbing. I was ready for one day in which only good things happened. The familiarity of pushing the mop across the linoleum tile gave me an escape. The motion allowed me to leave my everyday life and launch into TV shows and movies. I wanted to find one moment when everything was so true, so perfect, that the movies couldn't do a better job. On the darkened highway, lights flashed by. Sometimes I wish I had gotten in the car with Julie.

* * *

The roads on the way home emptied. The street lamps provided limited light, enough to make the hollow feeling around me distinct. One or two cars joined me as I approached my house. The house enrobed in the shadows of neighboring trees and homes. A cat raced by the side of the home and chased a squirrel.

My home wept from the dew that hung around the window frames. A sadness joined the shadows and they melded to form a coat that covered the building. I waited before it, not sure what I waited for. Maybe I hoped that the blanket would be removed and the house would smile back at me. The way it had smiled when we returned from Sunday service when I was little and the smell of waffles came through the kitchen window. Growing up, I had been greeted by the sound of talk shows and sitcoms. I liked to hear them as I walked in. It felt like I had company and brought life into the house. Tonight I wanted to crawl into bed and hide. Even from my home and all it held. This house knew I was alone.

I crossed the threshold, took off my coat and tossed it over the dining room table. I wanted to go straight to bed and become lost under the covers, but my mind still ran with the day's events. I wandered into the kitchen while carrying a bag of leftovers Mrs. P had given me. Maybe dad would like them. I knew without checking that he wasn't home.

I stripped off my uniform and put it where my other uniform hung, inside the small white metal washer near the back door. I crawled into my bathrobe, enjoying the feeling of soft cotton as it draped my arms and wrapped my body. I tied it tightly closed and knotted it shut. My body and mind drained. My favorite magazine, *Entertainment This Month*, had arrived with the day's mail. I tore through the pages to find news about Jonathan.

I couldn't let the Ps know how excited I was. Jonathan Pearce here? I dreamt about it sure but I didn't think I'd see him in person so soon. Ever since I was a teenager, I had sent him letters telling him how much I loved his movies and how great he was.

I rolled up the magazine and put it in my bathrobe pocket. I snuggled into an overstuffed armchair. I fanned my hair along the back of the chair and sat with my legs folded underneath. Before me the television hummed. The remote felt heavy and big in my hands. With the next channel came my favorite interview show. The host, Lawrence Corran, spoke with Jonathan. I couldn't believe it. They played a rerun of my favorite episode.

The two men were on a stage with a black backdrop. On a table next to them stood glasses filled with water. Lawrence, a small man with a receding hairline, thick horn-rimmed glasses, a goatee, and a rounded jaw, sat across from Jonathan. Jonathan lounged in his high backed chair. If someone else sat in the chair, it would have been overpowering, but he looked confident, relaxed. Mama used to call him a young Sean Connery. His thin black sweater provided a hint of the muscles underneath it. A grey suit jacket hung from his shoulders. The creases in his black suit pants followed the bend of his knees. I wanted to reach in and touch those creases. He glowed with each move and every word. He crossed his legs and formed a pyramid with his fingers.

"Wasn't that screen test for the next day?"

Jonathan looked embarrassed by the question. "Yes. They said they could use someone with my looks and then sent me home."

I moved closer to the screen.

"How long after that test did you get your first part?"

"Six months."

"Now. See students? Don't get discouraged if they don't call you back immediately. Even Jonathan Pearce waited to get his first part." Lawrence flipped to the next note card.

"I was an extra in a military movie called, *The Edge of Life*."

My lips moved in time with his.

"I had one line. I said, 'Sir, yes sir.'" His eyes crinkled with a touch of a smile. I had heard this story a dozen times.

"Again, students. Not only did he have to wait six months but he also had a very small role."

"After that my next role wasn't for another year. I took night classes and got a job as a construction worker."

"That's how you stayed trim."

"I wanted to spend my money on classes so I needed a job that would maintain my physique." Jonathan turned, looked at me and leaned in. "Lauren. Lauren? How are you doing?"

I looked around the living room. I felt self-conscious in my clothes. I tied the knot in my robe tighter and pointed to myself as if another Lauren sat next to me.

"Yes. I wondered if you needed anything?" he said.

I hesitated for a moment. My throat dried up as I tried to respond. "I-I-I'm fine."

Jonathan rested back in his chair, tension eased from his shoulders. "Good. I'm glad to hear it. I'll be in town soon. We can get together for coffee."

Did Jonathan Pearce ask me out on a date? "I'm sorry? I mean. Sure. That. Would. Be. Great." I reached my hand out to touch the screen. To see if I could be there with him and test if this was real. My fingertips reached the screen's edge. The static electrified them, covered them in a fuzzy haze that spread up my wrist and traveled down my arm. It prepared me to become one with the images before me. Ready me to become one with Jonathan. I prepared to break through the barrier of static, glass, and electricity, when Jonathan said, "Lauren, you better get to bed." He nudged my shoulder. "I gotta go now. Don't forget. Coffee." He winked. "Lauren. Lauren?" His voice changed to emulate my father's tone. Now that's a gross thought. Someone shook my shoulder a little more. A fog broke free from my mind. It forced me to wake up. The television shone before me, my father clicking off the static filled screen. "You should head to bed now."

"Right. Thanks, Dad." He seemed unusually lucid at this hour. It must have been three in the morning.

"I'm feeling like tomorrow'll be a good day," he said. He headed into the common bathroom. "I'm feeling a lil lucky."

"Me too," I said. "Me too."

Chapter 3

We began the weekend with a visit to Mrs. P's advisor. The woman had provided guidance to my boss since she first moved to the United States. Mrs. P swore by her accuracy.

"Besides," she said. "Can't hurt to ask."

A cracked and lifted path led to Nuri the seer's, home. We never spoke about why Mrs. P needed to see her other than tradition, or why these trips seemed important, but Mrs. P invited me to come with her on occasion.

Outside Nuri's house glowed a sign, *Walk-Ins Welcome. $10 Initial Reading* along with the silhouette of a woman wearing a red scarf. She gazed into a crystal ball as her hands hovered over it. Star shaped deck lights lined the windows and doorway of the Colonial. Every other lightbulb had burnt out, the rest flickered and glowed as if they had tried to make up for the neighboring lights.

As we crossed the entryway into the house, I could feel the change from the outside to the inside, like an emotional dampness had come over us the moment we stepped foot onto the grey carpet. No sunlight invaded the house due to the heavy velvet curtains. Sconces with blazing candles lined the mirrored wall behind the seer. The air had become thick with the prominent smell of wax.

"You come again?" She squatted in her wide mahogany glazed chair behind a round cocktail table covered in a patchwork cloth of reds, yellows, and shades of black. The stitching contrasted the patches of color, black with yellow stitching and red with black stitching. This created a pattern of paths that ended on one patch and bled into another. "You want to know more," she said. "Come. Sit." She watched as we approached. It felt creepy when she did this, like she was sizing us up. The outline of her clothes and face blended into the beginnings of the candlelight. When she moved, the lines became even hazier.

Mrs. P looked like she bowed before Nuri as she leaned into her chair. I held my purse in my hands ready to leave. I didn't want the seer to think that I believed everything she predicted. Nuri's voice got a little huskier each time we met, like she fought a continuous cold.

"I see you're still skeptical, Lauren," she said. "You're still searching."

I thought of what my mama taught me; that I should have faith in God. I wondered if being here negated my faith.

"Lauren, have respect for Nuri." Mrs. P whispered and poked me in the side with her finger. Nuri smiled with the comment. I wanted to ask about my mom and find out where she was. Find out if my dad's prediction was right.

"I knew you would be coming." Nuri wore clothes made from thrown away scarves to create a fluid, multicolored dress that covered her body and flowed over her head.

The fluidity reminded me of the way the trees swayed in the fall breeze the last time my dad and I had visited my mom's grave. One of the few moments I knew my father would be at my side. Every Sunday he took flowers to my mama. That day the sky filled with rain and quiet. I used to use these moments to talk to my dad. To find out how his week went. To see if he needed anything. He was always sure to show up sober. As if the one day of dryness made up for the week of being checked out.

"We need to know. What will happen with the visitors?" Mrs. P folded a twenty-dollar bill into a handkerchief and put it under the crystal ball's base.

Mrs. P referenced Jonathan. What did he want from us? From me?

The seer closed her eyes and sat back. "You need to know about the movie?"

My mind jumped back and forth. There had been so much change and so much pain. I thought about Mama and when she had died. I had been so mad at Dad for not looking out for her. I couldn't take it anymore and screamed and screamed at him for being a horrible father and a terrible husband. I locked myself in my bedroom and watched one movie after another. I didn't bother to answer the door when he knocked.

"Yes. We need to know about the movie." Mrs. P's eyes glittered.

I only felt guilty when the knocking stopped. After I had calmed down I found my father in his room crying over my mother's photos. He had looked so small. He had stayed small.

Mrs. P nudged me and nodded toward the seer. "Pay attention," she said. The old woman tapped the handkerchief and slid it into her lap. She waved her hands around the crystal ball.

And then I thought of Jonathan. His face. His smile. His laugh. His feel. And a warmth grew; one that drew the pain away. Just like every time I heard his voice. Somehow he showed up when I needed him most.

"Oh but the spirits want to talk. I can feel them in the room. They are here and they want to share but. But . . ."

"But?" Mrs. P moved closer to the seer as if this action helped 'tune in' the spirits. Her chair rubbed against the hardwood flooring. I wanted to hear from the spirits, my spirits, even though they visited me at home. I stiffened in my seat.

"They're missing something. Something." She slid the empty handkerchief across the table.

Then I remembered where I was. I was before an elderly woman whom we had known for years. Not before a real seer. Not before someone who could judge or know what went on in my life.

"Something?" Mrs. P asked. She didn't notice the bright white cloth that jutted from the table. I nudged Mrs. P and nodded toward the handkerchief. "Oh. I see." Mrs. P dug through her purse to find another bill and slid it across.

"They are here." Nuri grazed the crystal ball with the tips of her pointed fingernails. "You will have much success from this. You will have many visitors. Some will be good and some will be bad." She looked up from the ball and tried to get my attention.

I looked away. For a moment, I was afraid that she could see inside my mind. Once I looked away, I shook off this feeling but I was sure not to look up again. I didn't need to be here. I knew why Jonathan was coming. I knew where my parents were.

"One will stand out. He will attract the young one. He will bring much joy but in the end much sorrow. You must decide if the elation is worth the anguish." She eased back into her chair and looked up to the ceiling. "The signal. It is weaker now. The spirits need more help."

Mrs. P looked at me and smacked me under the table. "So?"

"What? I don't have any money." I wanted to go home or at least away from there. I clutched my purse closer to my chest, ready to leave. This was ridiculous. I didn't know why I gave in whenever Mrs. P asked me to come with her.

"Fine." Mrs. P took a ten-dollar bill from her pocket and put it under the crystal ball's stand.

"Yes. I see now." The seer went through the same routine with the handkerchief and waved her hands around the crystal ball. "He will be handsome and he will make her feel like she is the only woman on earth. But this is not so. She's searching for something that was lost but he won't find it."

I built up a wall. One that wouldn't let me hear everything she said. An invisible wall that let me stay distant from the predictions. A wall that kept me away from the words and what they might have meant. I didn't need her words. I knew the truth.

"What about the movie? Will it be good?" Mrs. P asked.

"The movie will be great and the diner will become famous. First there will be some confusion." She tipped her hands back and forth. "It will be replaced with happiness." She slouched. "The spirits are tired."

"Thank you, Nuri," Mrs. P said. She got up and headed for the door. I leapt from my seat. Mrs. P took her shawl and wrapped it around her shoulders. I readied to cross the threshold, return to the real. I held my worn soft leather bag to my side. The seer began again.

"Lauren. You have other questions you want to have answered, but the answers are only for you. Spirits wait to talk to you. When you're ready, tell me."

I hovered my foot over the doorjamb. I shivered with her words. I wanted to tell her to kiss off, leave me alone but instead I said "Thanks," and turned away. As we walked down the broken cement path the cracks in the pavement healed as we neared the diner. I shook off the seer's words as Mrs. P talked on and on, reflecting on the seer's predictions.

I thought of what I should have said to the seer. I wanted to tell her that I'd spoken to the spirits. I should have said that if I wanted to talk to them I could go home and sit in her bedroom. She'd conjure images from our past and tell me more than any seer could. She'd laugh with me as we talked and I'd ask her what to do about work or love or life. Then I'd sit alone in the solitude of her bedroom and feel the still air around me as she returned to their new home. I'd tell Nuri that I didn't need her and her predictions, her fake words, her false self. I was truer than anyone or anything she could ever try to conjure. "Come, Lauren," Mrs. P lead the way to the diner. "We have work to do."

Chapter 4

Chatter filled the small space of the Oaklyn Diner. Every booth, every stool, every inch contained someone. In the midst of the visitors Mrs. P wandered from table to table. She poured coffee and discussed God-knows-what.

"What's going on?" I asked Mr. P who read a newspaper behind the register. I eased my way to him as he continued to read. I think he was trying to be invisible. The phone rang. I reached for it when Mrs. P's head jerked and she practically ran over customers.

"No, no. I got it." She yanked the receiver off the wall. The coil jumped into the air and smacked my hand.

"Mrs. P. She call everybody." Mr. P spoke behind the paper.

"We'll make this place famous." Mrs. P announced into the telephone. She must have been speaking to family because she looked animated when she gossiped with her cousins. She glanced in my direction and did a double take. "I got to go. Lauren's here." She hung up and turned to me. "What do you think?"

"About what?" I asked.

On my way to the restaurant, I anticipated a quiet day before the film crews came. I wanted to look through my magazines and catch *Entertainment This Month* and *Celebrity Tonight* to make sure I had the latest scoop. Don't misunderstand me. I couldn't wait to see Jonathan. In fact, I barely slept the night before. I lay in bed studying Jonathan's poster from his first pirate movie, *The Last Ghost Ship*. He wore a captain's uniform that made his shoulders seem even broader and stronger, and the jacket's grey fabric crystallized his blue eyes. Deanna Cartridge, his romantic interest, clutched his arm from behind. Her peasant dress torn and hanging from her shoulders. The tattered ghost ship in the background. I could still hear him say, "*Only for you*," my favorite line in the movie.

Mrs. P motioned to the restaurant. "About all this. The film. Your favorite guy." She winked.

"I don't know. I guess this is all right," I said.

"You see," Mr. P interjected. "Lauren's more like me. She needs to see to believe."

Mrs. P waved him off. "This is more than all right." She surveyed the room. "Word spread." She scrunched her eyebrows and wrinkled her nose like she smelled something bad. When I didn't respond, she relaxed. "I made a few phone calls and offered free coffee."

"See Lauren," Mr. P said. "She made a few phone calls. That's my love, she makes things happen." He pointed at the silver coffee makers and the empty carafes. On each station, clusters of coffee cups poised for more. The talking became louder and more animated with each sip.

"Time to make more," Mrs. P said.

The diner felt cramped. "But where will our regulars sit? What if they want it to be quiet?"

Mrs. P waved me away.

"But—" I continued.

"It-is-fine-it-is-fine." Over her shoulder she ordered. "Don't stare at me. Check on those tables." She flicked her arm in the air and refilled the coffee maker with fresh grounds. "Well?" she questioned.

"Right. I'll get to it." I grabbed my notepad from under the counter and approached the nearest table. "May I help you?"

The temperature in the Oaklyn Diner had risen from the large number of bodies. This place wasn't meant to have this many people jammed in at one time, no matter how much room had been added.

"Would you like to order?" I asked a slight man with wire-rimmed glasses.

"Nah. We're fine. When is the movie crew coming? Do you think they will film today? You know, in high school I was in *Our Town*. I knew then that I belonged in the movies." His eyes sparkled with the word *movies*. His wife quietly played with their daughter. She jingled a soft plastic toy with bright greens, yellows, and blues.

"I don't think they're coming today. Maybe in a day or two," I said and tucked my notepad into my pocket.

They exchanged looks.

"Did you hear that?" He turned to the guy in the booth next to him. "She said they aren't coming today."

The man, a young guy with black hair and black-brown eyes replied. "Mrs. Polyxena didn't say they would film today. She said they might scout. Can't hurt, you know. The more we're around, the more likely we'll be extras. Right, Lauren?"

"Sure."

The next thing I knew it felt like someone hit stop on a VCR. All sound disappeared, well, except for the guy in glasses who said, "I bet they pick me to be an extra. I'll even get a speaking role." Because of the immediate silence he sounded like he had spoken at triple the normal volume. Much of the crowd had turned to watch a man wearing black biker shorts approach the register.

"What's this?" Mrs. P questioned.

The biker's dark hair shot out from underneath a helmet as beads of perspiration ran down his face. He eyed a glass of water on the counter, his chest heaved as he tried to slow his breathing. He looked like he had jumped Mount Rushmore to get us the package.

"I don't know, lady. All I know is they made me bring this over. Sign here." He shoved a clipboard with line after line of names and dates. She scribbled her name on the bottom of the page.

"Thanks." He took one last look at the glass, and then with his ten-speed on his shoulder he asked Mrs. P to call a cab for him. "I need a better job," he said. Mrs. P handed him the water and gave him a bag of bear claw pastries.

"How much do I owe you?" he asked.

She hung up with the cab company and said to him, "Nothing. Consider it a tip."

The delivery guy shook her hand and headed out the door while he pulled a bear claw from the bag.

Mr. P looked at his wife over the top of his newspaper. "Alexandra?"

"Don't start," she said.

"Since when do we give food away?"

"He was bony and they were two days old," she said.

Outside, the delivery guy devoured the last of the pastry and then wrestled to get his bike onto the top of the cab rack.

Mr. P nodded. "Some days I think you'll be the death of me," he said.

"More like the life."

"What did you say?" he asked.

I picked up the package. "I asked what this is."

Mrs. P read the envelope. "Nothing important. Mr. P and I will look at it." She took the package from me, walked up to her husband and placed a hand on his shoulder. "Come on, Mister.

We have work to do." He finished the article and the two disappeared into his office. I imagined them opening the package to find a note from Jonathan addressed to me, then they burst out of the office while Mrs. P waved the note, "*It's for you! He needs to see you right away.*" Mrs. P would hug me and Mr. P would shake my hand. *"I always knew he was your guy."*

"Excuse me. Miss?" A customer at table eight called to me. He lifted his coffee mug and nodded. The crowd returned to a low roar. The short lived excitement gone with the delivery man.

I returned to my tables and waited for the Ps to return. After a bit, I decided that they needed a break and maybe a snack. I poured two cups of coffee and picked up a cruller, Mr. P's favorite, knocked on the office door and entered to find them huddled over a stack of papers, the package ripped open.

"I thought you could use this." I put the mugs on the table and Mr. P reached for the pastry.

"You already had one today," Mrs. P said.

"True, but this is a special day. Thank you, Lauren." He bit into the donut before she could take it from him.

"I was talking to Rich and he mentioned something about how movie folks might cause a lot of damage." Rich and I saw the same exposé on what happens behind the scenes. He had stopped by a little earlier to ask if I had seen the same special. "I'm sure they can handle it," I had told him, but then the contract came and I wasn't so sure. Behind me someone asked for a waitress. "I'll be right there," I called back, hoping that our part-timer would help him.

"I see that," said Mrs. P. She skimmed to a section of the contract. "We're absolutely taking this to our lawyer, Xavier. He'll be by later." She glanced up at me. "Don' worry. We'll be fine," Mrs. P said. "Go back and check on the tables."

* * *

I scraped bits of leftover meatloaf special from the plates and avoided looking at the congealed globs and grease laden fries. The cold smell of old food made my stomach turn. I never minded cleaning or serving but the one chore I couldn't stand was scraping old food off of people's plates. The food wasn't good enough for a doggy bag. Covered in perspiration, I had an odd chill while working in a room that otherwise felt like a hundred degrees hotter than usual.

Turned out Dad's luck had changed; he had gotten a job unloading products from docked ships and prepping boxes for distribution. The first shipment contained bananas. He never saw spiders so big. I didn't ask anything else about his day.

Masses of conversation continued to fill the diner. The bells above the front door tinkled. I longed for the days before all of this, when I could relax in the solitude. My first thought was to tell whoever came in that we had a full house and they should come back tomorrow.

I wiped my brow with the back of my wrist and peered through the breezeway to find Mrs. P embracing a man three times her size. A round man, one cheesesteak away from not being able to button his pants, Xavier loved Mrs. P's cooking and looked for any reason to visit. I couldn't help but smile at him. He reminded me of Santa Claus.

"Lauren." Mrs. P called for me to bring Xavier his favorite dishes, something I didn't mind doing. His arrival meant I was closer to seeing Jonathan. I stacked the platters from my forearm to my wrists and backed my way to his table, careful not to let the back spring of the door force me and the platters to fling forward onto the patrons.

"Lauren." His smile had grown since the last time I saw him. "You know what I like." He waved me to him and made room for the dishes on the table.

"We always ready for you, Xavier. Always ready." Mrs. P took the food from my arms and placed the plates before him.

"Miss, when you have a second!" A woman at the neighboring table called. I hadn't talked to Xavier since he'd been here weeks prior and I wanted to find out more about his business and the contract.

"Lauren. You go ahead and help them. We can talk more later," Mrs. P suggested.

I raced to the table and refilled the drinks, half-heard the customers as they asked for the check. I was too busy trying to hear Xavier's conversation. I checked in here and there to see if Xavier needed anything. Mrs. P waved me off. I never got back to talk to him. The next thing I knew, the evening came and we were closing up. Of course, I "volunteered" for the overly glamorous job of mopping up.

I found another smooshed something or other underneath a table. It may have been a potato but now it had track marks and ketchup and another color that looked like mold caught in the imprint. Normally Mrs. P asked one of us waitresses to mop the floor every other day, but because of the huge number of people that ran through this place, she changed it to every day. I mopped crushed food and sticky spilt drinks that attracted bits of dust and dirt that entered the diner. "I don't even know what this is," I mumbled. The last customer had left an hour before.

Mr. P returned to the backroom and said he had more work to do. Dotty had left right after we closed, and after balancing the register Mrs. P sent Monica to the bank with the day's cash and checks, since the bank was on her way home. Mrs. P wiped the counter and finished the last bit of cleaning. "You know what? This. This is good."

"What's good?" I locked the front door and turned the Open sign to Closed. I hoped she didn't reference finding one hundred year old crusty ketchup. The day had swiftly turned to night.

"This. This diner, these people, these friends. What we're doing." I wanted to tell her they weren't our friends. We had something they wanted, and I didn't think a single one of them cared about us. The more she talked, the harder it was not to tell her the truth. I focused on a smudge on the counter. The cloth squeaked against the faux marble and in the silence between us. I thought about acting optimistic by telling her I was sure everything would change for the better with the movie, even though I was sure she thought everything already had changed.

Someone knocked on the door. I looked up to find a tall figure with his hands before his eyes as if they were a magnifying glass.

"Lauren, can you get that?" Mrs. P rested on a counter stool, a pencil in hand, and a lined notepad before her. The contract had been signed and sent. The crew would arrive the following week. Who knew what waited for us? I wondered if I would be able to get near the diner. I navigated the newly mopped floor to the front door.

"I'll be right there," I yelled. Who wanted something to eat at ten at night? The closer I got, the clearer I saw the figure. His faded brown corduroy jacket looked like it had been worn a thousand times. Patches of leather covered the elbows and pockets. Their softness hung on the wearer's skin. The jacket was accompanied by black pants and black leather shoes, the kind of shoes that a formal man wears when he tries to look casual. He knocked one more time when he saw me. Weird. He wore sunglasses.

"I'm almost there." I wiped my eyes with the backs of my hands. I tried to avoid getting cleaning fluid in them. I wondered if I'd be allowed to stay on set while the movie filmed. Mr. Smarthey didn't say we had to leave and he didn't say we could stay. I had started to question if I'd meet Jonathan. As I unlocked the deadbolt I looked up. "I'm sorry, we're closed."

"I just wanted to stop by and introduce myself." He moved his hand into the door's opening. I followed the length of him, which led me to his eyes hidden behind the dark frames. "I'm Jonathan Pearce."

For whatever reason, what he said didn't immediately register. Maybe I watched his mouth too closely or the scent from the cleaning fluid made me too lightheaded or maybe I was tired from the day, but I repeated those words in my head before they finally registered. *I'm Jonathan Pearce. I'm Jonathan, Pearce. I'm. Jonathan. Pearce.* And then it hit. I couldn't imagine what I looked like to him. Other than the fact that I was covered in cleanser and stank of garbage and artificial lemons. I wasn't sure if I should hide, hug him, scream in delight, or run far, far away. I couldn't seem to find the right place for my hands or my eyes. Suddenly everything felt awkward and out of place.

In the movies his face was illuminated. In person, he glowed. I traced each line of his face and verified that this wasn't another dream. The thickness of his black lashes, the slope of his nose. One dimple accentuated when he smiled. The angle of his jaw that brought me to the length of his neck. I wanted to reach out and touch him, just like before. This time if I did, this would be real. I'd know the softness of his coat, the strength of him against the fabric. The feel of his skin, smooth and firm. My mouth opened and then closed. I wanted to tell him that he'd found me. All of this in seconds. Only the sounds of passing cars entered through the doorway.

"I hear I'm gonna spend a bit of time here. I wanted to take a moment to meet everyone." I moved out of Jonathan's way so he could come in. He offered his hand and held mine like a true gentleman. I felt lightheaded and grabbed his hand tighter so not to fall. Then I realized I had stopped breathing and deeply inhaled. "Hi," he said.

What was I supposed to say? I simply said "hi," in a voice I didn't recognize. One that was squeaky and small.

Mrs. P looked up. "Who is it, Lauren?" She wrote line after line on her pad. "If he needs to make a call then we have a phone. No coffee. No food, but we have a phone and ice water if he wants." When she turned to see him, she narrowed her eyes, "You look like—"

He winked at me and then headed to her. He moved the same way he did in television shows and movies, like his shoes never touched the floor. He removed his glasses as he approached her. The skin at the tips of his eyes wrinkled when he smiled.

"You're the Pearce guy. See Lauren. What did I say?" She shook his hand.

Nuri predicted that someone famous would visit and change our lives. I knew from Mrs. P's look that we would trek to the seer again.

"Yup. You were right." I couldn't take my eyes off of him. I thought that he'd disappear if I did. I almost reached out to pinch him. Instead, I pinched my inner arm.

"You were expecting me? I asked the scouting agency not to let you know. Sometimes when people find out I'm coming. Well . . ." He laughed. I laughed with him. An uncertain, nervous laugh. "You are Mrs. Polyxena? I hear you're quite an interesting lady."

Mrs. P fluttered her eyelashes. "I'm not very interesting."

"I think what I heard is true." He kissed her hand. I wanted him to touch mine again. Then he turned, "And you must be Lauren. They told me you were beautiful but I don't think they did you justice."

I held back the comment, *yeah right*. Instead I thanked him. Maybe he made it up but why would he do that? I accepted his hand and squirmed in place. I wanted to run away. I wasn't used to someone paying so much attention to me. "It is a pleasure to meet you, Mr. Pearce," I said.

"Call me Jonathan."

I couldn't let go of his hand. He didn't release mine. We stood there for what felt like hours. We stared at each other. His eyes were so blue.

"Who was knocking on the door? Did you say we're closed?" Mr. P came out from the backroom. His comment snapped me from my trance. Without looking away, Jonathan responded. "Hello. You must be Mr. Polyxena. I have heard wonderful things about your restaurant."

"Why yes, this is a wonderful restaurant. And you need what? You need a phone? You need water?" Jonathan looked confused. Mr. P escorted him to the front door, which forced Jonathan to let go of my hand.

"Oh darleeng, no. This is Jonathan Pearce. He came to say hello." Mrs. P went to her husband's side.

"Who? Lauren, isn't he the guy you like?"

My face grew hot. I couldn't move. I mumbled. Nothing important. I just mumbled.

"You're funny, dear. This is Jonathan. He'll be starring in the movie." She pulled on her husband's shirt sleeve.

Mr. P looked at me and then at Jonathan, who by this time must have been ready to leave. He must have thought "*here is a psycho lady who reads star magazines and ogles me. What a mistake to come here.*"

"Welcome to our restaurant." Mr. P offered his hand to Mr. Pearce.

"Pleasure to meet you." They shook hands. "I don't need anything. I like to introduce myself before the film crew comes and we get caught up in the movie. I wanted to thank you in advance for hosting this film."

Mrs. P came from behind her husband and approached Jonathan. She looked at me with a warning.

"You know. Lauren'd be good in this movie. She's cute. Just look at those eyes. Have you ever seen such brilliant grey-green eyes? And those pouty lips. The kind every man wants to kiss." Mrs. P rambled about how I needed to do something with my life and waitressing wasn't it. "She's better than serving."

"She exaggerates," I demurred. I couldn't look at him. I was too embarrassed by Mrs. P's words. I prayed she would stop.

"We'll can see what we can do," Jonathan said. He rested against the counter. "I am sure we can use at least one attractive woman in this movie." He winked at me. "It's getting late. I don't want to keep you from your work." He shook Mr. and Mrs. P's hands and said, "It was an honor to meet you both." Then he offered his hand to me again. "And to the beautiful Lauren. It was a pleasure." He lifted my fingers and brushed them against his lips. He looked at me through the kiss, a grin in his eyes.

He left as quickly as he had entered. Mr. and Mrs. P remained in front of the swinging doors. I fixated on my hands. I still felt the warmth of his breath, the gentleness and safeness of his touch. I replayed him calling me beautiful. Bee-UUU-tiful. He could say it a thousand times. Beeee-uuuuu-tiful. Beu-tifl.

Chapter 5

A silver van with a satellite dish pointed to the clouds sat parked across the street from the Oaklyn Diner. Crewmembers ran from the van to the restaurant with their arms full of wires, screens, and boxes. It reminded me of a colony of bugs trying to make the queen bee happy.

Since Jonathan's visit, I had trouble sleeping. My dream filled nights had turned to nightmares. After last night, I was ready for the daylight. I needed to have a little bit of reality blended into my life. I pulled my hair away from my face, the strands still wet from showering. I barely entered when a man wearing jeans and a t-shirt saying "f-this" directed me through the diner. He had George Michael stubble and highlighted hair. He led me to a tent that had been set up in the front of the diner.

"Honey. I'm going to need you to go over here. We'll be a little while." He glanced at me for a second. A second longer than I was comfortable and then smiled. The Ps sat on folding chairs underneath the makeshift structure, the type of chairs with the word "director" or "star" on the back. They watched the crew scurry by.

"Is it okay if I go over there?" I pointed to the Ps. I hoped he'd say yes so I could escape the madness.

"Sure," he said. "You can go over there. Be careful of the wires." I swear he looked me up and down but he did it so quickly, I wasn't quite sure and then he turned to walk away.

"Wires? What?" A mass of black, red, and blue wires layered the ground. They led to light fixtures or equipment or stands. Wires disappeared behind furniture and underneath tent flaps and snaked through windows while others traveled to nowhere. Next to the diner, a large power generator hummed.

"Mrs. P?" I made my way to them. "What's going on?"

"They came early. They said they needed to set up for the actors." Mrs. P patted the arm of an empty chair next to her. "Come. Sit." I took my place next to her. The Ps had put in the contract that they could be present whenever they chose and they wrote me into it as well. Sometimes being the owners' favorite had its perks. Meanwhile Monica and Dotty decided to go on vacation. I glanced over to find Mr. P who looked ready to hide in his back office. He winced with the sounds of banging and crashing.

When I saw Mr. P wince I wanted to yell at them not to touch a picture or put a hole in the wall. I moved forward to do it. "Excuse me," I said to the closest person I could find. "Do you think you could—" He raced past me. I grabbed the next guy by the arm. "What are you doing?"

He yanked his arm away. On the back of his black nylon jacket was the word "crew."

"How much longer will this take?"

He shrugged. "Depends. Sometimes a day. Sometimes a couple of days. Sometimes longer. Depends on how much we need to change."

Mrs. P pulled on the back of my shirt. "It's okay. We agreed to this," she said. Her voice calmed but Mr. P didn't look at ease. His skin turned white and then a pale shade of green.

"Mr. P? Are you okay?" With each move and bang of the hammer, he looked sicker.

"Was that it?" The tech asked.

"Yeah. I guess . . ."

Mrs. P called me back to my place.

"We agreed." Mrs. P reminded her husband. "They'll put everything back when they're done." She touched his hand.

"My restaurant." He looked at Mrs. P. "Alexandra." His eyes widened.

"Darleeng. This is better. Remember, there's always sorrow before joy." She kissed him on the cheek, the magic potion that eased his tension. This time he became still; so still that I feared he had stopped breathing.

"You go home now. We'll be all right. We'll make sure everything's fine." The expression on Mrs. P's face changed from calm to concern.

"That's right. We'll make sure everything goes back to the way it was," I said.

"Call me if anything happens." He got up and wandered to the front door. I was afraid he wouldn't make it down the steps. He looked so lost, so helpless. I had never seen him like this.

Mrs. P whispered to me, "I'm going with him. Stay here and make sure everything's all right." She exited before I could answer.

I watched the door, hoping to see Jonathan. I opened my mouth to ask what was going on. Ask someone if Jonathan was coming, but somehow the words never came until after the person passed. While getting the courage to ask, the man with the "f-this" shirt came up to me. "Excuse me. Are you Lauren?"

"Uh yeah," I said.

"Good," he said. "I'm Zachary." He offered his hand, his grip firm, and continued to talk. "I was told to talk to you."

"Nice to meet you."

"This is probably traumatic for Mr. and Mrs. Polyxena. I wondered if you could talk to them?" He continued and sat in the chair next to me. He leaned closer as if sharing a secret. Although his presence was professional, something about him made me want to talk to him. Maybe it was his hazel eyes or the fact that underneath his calm and matter-of-fact exterior, he seemed like a kind person.

To be honest, I wasn't sure if I wanted to stick around, no matter how much I loved the movies, but I knew I couldn't leave. I promised the Ps that I'd stay. "We will put everything back the way we found it. But for a while this place is going to be rearranged."

He looked honest enough. I didn't have a reason not to believe him. If movie crews pummeled every location they went to then I doubted they could continue making movies. "What can I do?"

He placed his hand next to mine. Our fingertips touched. "Reassure them, would you? I hear you are the heart and soul of this place." He snapped his minty gum. "Is that true?"

"Oh no. That's the Ps. They live for the Oaklyn."

"You're at least the backbone." He tilted his head for a moment and then searched through a folder and looked at me again. "I know the Polyxenas. Wait, did I say that right?"

I nodded. "Close enough."

"They had mentioned to Jonathan about having you in the film, which is entirely *un*orthodox." He said unorthodox like the word was taboo. "But, they definitely asked the right person. So."

"So?"

"How do I put this?" This time he flopped the folder into his lap and then put his hand over mine. "The girl we have playing the waitress isn't very good. Or rather, she would be good if she wasn't such a . . ." He looked away and then looked back as if the word he wanted not only escaped him but had run far away. "Your friend's request was quite fortuitous. We could use your help."

I thought that actors were really waitresses or something like that. Isn't that an old joke? "I don't get it," I said.

"You want to make a few extra bucks?"

"Sure."

"Stand up a sec," Zachary said. I looked at him and he motioned for me to move. "It won't hurt. I just need to see something."

I got up and stood in front of him.

"Twirl," he said.

"You're kidding, right?"

"Just do it."

So, I twirled.

"That's fine. Good enough."

I hurried back to my chair.

"He was right about the eyes . . ." Zachary whispered and wrote something down in his folder.

"What was that?" I asked.

He closed the folder. "Nothing. Just thinking to myself. Here's the deal," he began. "The young lady who will be playing the waitress, which is a small but key role, had her mommy pay her way through college, school, life. Anyway, she needs some tips." From out of nowhere Zachary pulled a thick stack of bound pages with the word "CONFIDENTIAL" stamped on the cover. He waved at a crewmember across the room. "Here's a copy of the script, read through it and then go over the scenes with the girl."

"I can try. I never acted so I don't know how much of a help I'll be."

He plopped it into my arms. The script weighed more than a stacked tray.

"This isn't about acting. It's about realism. That's why we need your help. You're a real waitress and this one just doesn't get it." He smirked. "If I could get ten cents for every time one of these *actresses* thought they could *feel* their way through a part. I'd be a zillionaire. Then give me a dime for every time they were *wrong*. Oh. I'd be . . ." He stopped. "Start reading."

I had opened the cover and started flipping through the pages.

"Good. I knew you'd be the right person for the job. We'll pay you for your time. You can be our 'Resident Expert on Serving.' Ya know, like a martial arts expert."

"Fun," I said. Not sure if this really would be fun. Shock was a more accurate term. I couldn't believe I was on a set in the middle of New Jersey reading a confidential script for a movie starring the one man in the world I loved more than life. I told myself not to think about it otherwise I'd pass out. I skimmed through each page. What a great story. My body suddenly awoke with a rush of adrenaline. At some point my body would crash from the lack of sleep, but for that moment, I couldn't have been more awake.

"Wait, don't I need to sign a contract or something?" I asked.

"Don't worry. I'll take care of it. That's my job," he said.

Okay. This day turned out more interesting than I could have imagined.

"Have that read by tomorrow. I'll quiz you then. George, I need to talk to you." Zachary called to a guy with white-white hair and tan-tan skin. "Tomorrow," he said to me and walked away.

I continued through the pages. After a bit, I felt my lids growing heavier. Now I understood why they wanted to use this diner. It's like someone had grown up here. Like the writer had lived and breathed it and then wrote a story with the diner as the main spot.

Jonathan approached me. "Hello again," he said. With the back of his hand he lightly touched my cheek. His fingers grazed against my skin. "I missed you," he said. He cupped my chin in his hand and stroked the side of my face with his thumb. I nudged my face into his palm and he pulled me closer. I dropped the script. It thudded to the ground. He embraced me right when I thought he was going to lightly kiss me on the lips, just like his lips had grazed my hand the night before. His hands caressed my back. His grip tightened. I tried to look behind me but he held my head closer to him. I tried to pull away. The tighter his grip, the more I wanted to see what lay beyond him.

"You are fine now. I'm here," he said. His voice was calm but this wasn't right. He didn't need to hold me like this.

"I want to see. I want to know." I pushed my arms against him. I nearly broke free, but then I realized that if I didn't pull away, I could stay in his arms forever. I stopped and relaxed. "I'm fine," I whispered. He snuggled his head next to mine. His breath brushed against my neck. It warmed and then cooled. Along came an icy breeze that swirled around us. Small shivers topped my head and raced down my spine. His hands became frigid. He released me. "No," I whispered. "No," I said louder as the swirling air froze. I was in the center of a vortex but instead of calmness, I found another storm. My arms tingled with electricity. I reached my hands out and stretched. From the tips of my hands came sparks that shot through the air. They spread when I wiggled my fingers and formed a web of electricity. I looked up and my body traveled forward, through the roof of the diner over the street, and then the town. I could see my home blocks away. I never realized how small it was or how it formed a perfect rectangle. Just beyond it was the Oaklyn Elementary School where I had spent much of my childhood. The building tan and rimmed with trees. Directly behind it lay the playground with swings and a sandbox. All of this had been enclosed in a wired gate. A little bit beyond that was the Kimmel Middle School where I had hidden on days when I just couldn't go home. The teachers let me stay as long as I wanted. I usually said I was doing homework but I think they knew better. And then there was the Woodrow Wilson High School. The four story cement building with slits for windows. The building overpowered the elementary and middle schools. The homes nearby shrank. I still winced when I saw the high school, even this far away. Streets spread and crossed along the way. The neighborhoods quiet. The people ant-like. Most streets directed to the Oaklyn Diner beneath me. Only one thick road, the highway, led to places I couldn't imagine. I knew many had taken that road and never come back. It's the one that Julie took.

Jonathan ran to the front lawn of the diner. He looked up and cupped his hands over his eyes. The swirls blocked his face from me. I shifted my weight and moved left and then right. I glided through the clouds. My arms grew cold. The electricity faded. I shook my finger to get it to start again. I wiggled my arms. Nothing. I made fists and tried to force the energy back. My limbs became ice cold. My core felt leaden. "Jonathan?" Below me his face became visible. His eyes darkened. He waved. I tried to wave back when I shot down toward him. His eyes widened and he ran back into the diner. The street emptied. I raced faster and faster. For fear of impact, I sealed my eyes shut. The ground became closer within seconds. Only grass and concrete below me to break my fall. I tightened my arms and legs around me. I curled tighter into a ball, anticipating the crash.

"Lauren. Lauren?" I opened my eyes. Zachary shook my arm. "What are you doing?" he asked.

"What?" I rubbed my eyes and blinked. I shook my head. The tent had grown dark. The crew had gone. Seemed as though only Zachary and I remained.

"You need sleep. Just not here."

I lifted my head to find a trickle of drool had smudged the pages. My face ached. "I'm, uh, it was a long night?"

"Uh huh. Long night." He helped me out of the chair. "Go home."

We exited the tent and he said good night. I started toward my home but couldn't resist the chance to see the changes to the diner. I wandered to the rear entry and used my trusty key to get inside.

The building had been nearly dark, with bare light bulbs that hung from the ceiling and illuminated corners of the room. The diner had seemed to grow to twice its size. The construction unfinished with partially deconstructed walls. Booths had been removed from their longstanding spots, leaving a row of three near the windows. The underfloor visible where the booths had been. Planks criss-crossed over the openings. I tried not to step into the underside of the flooring. The room and all of its shadows moved as the moon hid behind clouds. The breeze had returned and rattled the windows, lightly whistling through the door opening. And so it began.

Chapter 6

I turned the corner to find a living cloud pushing and shoving to get closer to the Oaklyn.

The street had been blocked off to allow room to house the moving city including the director's and actors' trailers, production equipment, a tent for the director and his staff which is where we had been yesterday, a cafeteria truck, and costume and makeup trailers. All constructs dotted the street to form new paths between the standing homes and businesses. Each movement caused a ripple that pushed the cloud of people nearer to the diner's front door. Those closest to the building poured along the Oaklyn Diner's edges. Others snaked in between the buildings. They shoved forward, but half a block of people remained in their way. That didn't stop them from trying to get in. Police cars showed up, sirens blared. The cops came out with their hands on their sticks, chests puffed.

"I want to see him!" One woman wore an "I ♥ Jonathan" t-shirt cut up to reveal intimate areas of her body. She worked out a lot, evident from the fit of her tights. She shoved against the person in front of her.

I remained on the periphery, across the street and simply waited. Yesterday, I went home and studied the script, embarrassed about Zachary catching me in the middle of a daydream. I needed to concentrate. Last night, while I read the script, my mind wandered back to the dream and the feel of Jonathan and how he ran away.

A man in a coat, like the one Jonathan wore when he visited the diner before all heck broke loose, pushed his way closer to the front doors. He looked a little like Jonathan but meaner and with eyebrows that grew from the top of his nose and spread like wild bushes to each side of his head. He resembled a character Jonathan played in the sci-fi movie, *Blade Catcher*.

The guy ambled up to the police officer and tapped him on the shoulder. The officer acknowledged him.

"He knows me," the man told the cop.

"Who knows you?"

The guy sighed. "Jonathan Pearce."

"I'm sure he does, but first we need to get everything in order," the cop said.

They stood only a hundred feet away from me. Zachary had told me where I should meet him this morning but I forgot the note. I assumed it would be obvious when I got here. I thought about asking the officer for help. Maybe he'd know where I should go but based on the look on his face, I didn't think he was there to assist lost staff.

"You don't understand," the guy said. He started digging through his pockets.

While the officer was distracted I decided to find a way in on my own. More fans tried to talk, shove, or grope their way closer. I pushed through the mob and walked down the street, past empty storefronts and half-neglected rowhomes. I turned the corner to find the restaurant's rear entry. I hoped the cops hadn't blocked it. I wandered away from the crowd and followed the street behind the diner and then worked my way to the backyard. I stumbled through bunches of tall overgrown neglected weeds. The Ps didn't think they owned that part of the property and no one else wanted to claim it so the weeds remain untamed.

A rustling came from an overgrown bush. A woman crouched next to it.

"Hello?" I said.

"SSSHHHHssshhhhh. Don't let them know I'm here," she said. Her hair, tied back in a messy ponytail, looked like someone had attacked it with a bottle of hairspray and a teasing comb. Her dyed blonde strands reached her shoulder blades. The tops of her butt cheeks hovered above her jeans' top. "I don't want them to know I'm here," she whispered then returned to her hiding position.

"Okay." Not sure what to do about this, I left. I forced my way through the weeds. The brambles stuck to my jeans and shirt. When I made it out to the other side, I had been covered in stickers so I plucked them off. I reached the rear wooden fence that separated me from the diner.

A trash can helped to boost me over the fence. I jumped over and my arm jerked back forcing my backpack from me. My backpack had caught on a post and hovered above me leaving me to hang like a ragdoll from one of the arm straps. Needless to say, this was not a comfortable position. I thought my arms might rip from their sockets. I gave up trying to force myself free and hung limply from the fence.

Turned out I had leapt right next to another officer. "Come on," he said. He wore the standard uniform and looked disgusted like I was the twentieth person he'd found that day. I should have stayed home and watched television. The officer helped me shake free from my bag and fall to the dirt below.

I pointed to my backpack. "I. I need that. I'll just—" I wiped the dirt from my hands and got up to pull the bag free. I pulled and pulled. I must have tried too hard because next came a ripping sound from behind me. Pages from my journal, a plastic comb with missing teeth, a tube of lip gloss and the script showered the yard.

"Here ya go." In his hands were script pages. He read the cover and flipped through it. "Did you steal this?"

I had been gathering the other items and tossed the broken comb. I had just put them in the trash when he said this. He patted the pages.

"Steal? No," I said. I tried to think of another answer that he wouldn't think was contrived. The only explanation I had was the truth, but even I didn't believe it. "It was given to me." I started to explain why I had the script. He shook his head.

"Right. They want you to help an actress pretend she's a waitress. Who do you think I am?" He grabbed my arm causing it to shoot with pain. Great. What a wonderful day. I couldn't believe it. I hadn't gotten inside and already I was being taken away.

"Excuse me." A male's voice came from the diner's back door. I turned to find Zachary smoking a cigarette. He wore black on black, making his skin look even paler. "Thank you so much for being diligent. We appreciate how dedicated the officers have been in making sure that our cast and crew are safe, but that young lady belongs here." Zachary motioned to me. "She is here to act as a technical advisor." He took a long drag from his cigarette. He emphasized his words. "I am happy to take this young lady off your hands. I need her on the set." He looked at his wrist. "She *is* late."

"We've had a dozen people jump this fence since midnight. She makes thirteen." The officer let my arm go and handed me the script.

I couldn't look him in the eye. "Thank you," I said. I stuffed the last of my belongings into the bag and joined Zachary who had held his arms out to me.

"I wondered where you were," he whispered. "I forgot to tell you the code word." He treated the word "code" like it was the core of the sentence. He stubbed his cigarette on the concrete steps and led the way into the restaurant. We entered the diner. "What's even funnier about this fiasco is that Jonathan isn't here." He glanced at me, waited a beat, then waved it off.

I probably looked a wreck. My skin still itched from the brambles and my arms throbbed. I didn't want to raise them, otherwise I'd find out how much I'd really hurt them. "I know you won't say anything," Zachary said. He weaved through the kitchen and into the main dining area. Before me, people smacked against the windows as they tried to see inside the diner. Their clothes pressed against the glass, skin whitened from the force. Officers pulled the more fanatical ones and forced them into a police van across the street. One guy flailed at the officer and kicked his leg in the doorjamb. Another officer closed the door without noticing the guy's leg was in the way. Next thing we heard howling. I couldn't look any more. Within minutes sirens sounded and grew louder.

"No matter how many movies I'm a part of, I'm always surprised how crazy fans can be." He grabbed a box from the counter. "Here." He handed me the box. "This is the latest version of the script. I warned you it would change. These damn screenwriters always play with the scene. If you ask me, sometimes there isn't a whole lot they can do to make it watchable," he said. "You'll want to check this out. They expanded the waitress role. You sit over there and read. I'll be back when we need you." He pointed me to the nearest folding chair.

"Will Mrs. P be here today?" I asked. I hadn't talked to the Polyxenas since I saw them the day before. I knew I should have called.

"Oh right," he said. "She said something about stopping by later this afternoon. Why? Do you need her?"

"No. I'm fine. I just wanted to make sure . . . never mind."

* * *

I decided to take a break and get some food. The Oaklyn Diner's kitchen had been transformed into a set, meaning no cooking would occur until the filming was done. The best place to go was the catering truck stationed in the middle of the street. Mobs had left after the police showed in force and television crews appeared. I was happy to have my little corner of the diner. The catering woman wore a retro t-shirt with metal rivets forming a silver skull. Her hair was short spiky black with white-blonde highlights. She must have been my age.

"I told her she definitely needed to ditch the purple nail polish. I mean it's soooo eighties," the woman said to a customer. "You need something?" she asked me.

I hesitated. I felt like I'd showed up for a cocktail party dressed like a chicken. "What do you have for breakfast?"

"Whatever you want. We're like the army, always prepared," she said.

"Lena, that's not the slogan," said the customer on the other end of the nail polish conversation. He bit into an egg and cheese sandwich. The unnaturally yellow American cheese dripped from the side.

"It's close enough." Lena shone a white, full-toothed smile. Her lip gloss gave enough glint to spark the brightness of her teeth.

"Can I have some toast and jelly and maybe a cup of tea?" I peered into the truck. It reminded me of the street vendors in Philadelphia only bigger and with more food. Inside the truck was lined with metal and she had two burners behind her. Underneath the burners appeared to be an oven. To the left of this was an enormous refrigerator and next to that a freezer. The Ps would be jealous.

"That'll be the easiest order this morning." She came closer to me. "See that one over there?" She pointed to a woman sitting at a table under a white party tent. The woman had long dark hair in pigtails, oversized sunglasses—the kind in seventies movies—and a bedazzled white baby doll t-shirt. "She's one to look after. I've worked with her before. I predict she'll come to this cart every morning and ask for one thing, then when she gets it, she'll take one bite, spit it out and bitch that it's not what she ordered." The woman she pointed to silently gnawed on a piece of toast and read from a script.

"I never had a customer do that. People send their food back because they want it cooked more or less but never anything like that," I said.

"You a waitress?" She stepped back. "You must be that girl they hired to help out Little Miss Princess over there."

"Wait. You mean her?"

"You got it. Her name is Rane. She's the next best thing. The problem is she knows it."

Rane put down her toast and then shoved away a plate of half-eaten eggs and fruit. She flipped through the script and talked on her cell phone.

Lena wiped the counter and continued. "Make you a bet Little Miss Princess over there is talkin' to her agent and complaining how she had to be here before the stars." Lena looked at me and then slapped the countertop. The ketchup and mustard bottles jumped. "You wanted toast, right? I'll get that for you. By the way, I'm Galena but call me Lena."

"I'm Lauren." I reached over and shook her hand. "It's nice to meet you."

"Yeah. Nice to meet you too. It can get really boring around here." Lena disappeared into the back. Minutes later she popped out with two slices of thick browned toast and a small jar of marmalade. "I wasn't sure what kind of jelly you liked so I got you the good stuff. It's from my stash."

“Thanks. You didn’t have to do that.” It was the same kind of marmalade that had been Mama’s favorite. Which reminded me, I needed to check on Dad tonight. Seemed like everything was going well with the new job but I never knew.

“You’re going to have your hands full with that one. I thought a little bit of this might help you through the day.”

Another crewmember walked up and placed his breakfast order. Others moved on to their respective jobs.

I balanced the plate of toast and jam on my arm. I searched the area for a good place to sit. I didn’t want to sit next to Rane and she didn’t look like she wanted company. I started my way back to the diner.

“Hey you,” said a stern female voice. “Are you here to bring me my latte?” I turned to find Rane with her hand over the mouth of her cell phone. She pointed in my direction. There wasn’t anyone else near me.

“Me?” I asked.

“Yeah you. Why else would you be here?”

“Hey, *Ranie*. You best be good to her. She’s gonna teach you how to be common, ha.” Lena yelled and winked at me. “You know, since you don’t talk to the common peoples, we thought you could use a tutor.”

The guys in line at the catering truck snickered. I started my way back to the diner again, hoping this would end.

“I don’t know why *you* think this is so funny. How would I know she’s not part of the crew? She is well . . .” Rane swallowed the last word. “Let me call you back.” She spoke into the phone and immediately slammed it shut. She marched over to Lena. “Do *not* call me Ranie. You know I hate that nickname.” Then she looked at me like I was the most disgusting thing she had ever seen. “And you. *You*.” She pointed at my chest. “I am the one *you* will *listen* to.” She flitted a piece of hair out of her eyes.

I shifted my plate to my other hand. "I was asked to do a job. So, I'll do it. I didn't—"

"Ranie, I think you better back off. You have to work with her for God-knows-how-long this thing will take," Lena said.

"Don't call me Ranie!" She yelled over my shoulder and then stormed into a trailer. I looked around for other people's reactions. No one seemed to notice.

"Don't worry about her," Lena called over. "I'll tell you some stories later. But right now it looks like Mr. Wonderful is looking for you."

Zachary speed-walked to us. "What happened? All I heard was Queenie—I mean Rane—screaming." Zachary stopped in front of me. His question was clearly directed to me.

"To be honest, I'm not sure. I figured I'd get some toast and then I met Rane so . . ." I started to answer.

"Calm down. Lauren didn't do anything," said Lena. She had gotten out of the truck and leaned against its side. She lit a cigarette and blew a curl of smoke from the side of her mouth.

"You stay out of it. I wouldn't be surprised if you caused the commotion in the first place," said Zachary.

"You love me." She blew him a kiss and for a second, I swore he cracked a smile.

"Start talking," he said to me. I sighed and explained what had happened or at least what I thought happened.

"Figures," he said. "Listen. Rane is a spoiled, rotten brat but she is a pretty good actress. I don't think she knows how to do anything else. The director hired her for this bit part, mostly because her mom called in a favor." He looked at me like I had missed the point. "Do you know who Rane's mom is?"

I nodded. I had no idea who Rane's mom is. I had no idea who Rane was.

"Antonia Markoff," he said. "Rane doesn't know how to be normal and she clearly thinks she deserves attention since her mom was such a huge star. Don't take whatever she says personally. She can be a real bitch but you only have to deal with her for a few days. Feel sorry for those who have to deal with her on a regular basis. I'll get Queenie once she's cooled off."

Chapter 7

I sat down at the picnic table to eat my cold toast. Zachary had followed Rane into her trailer and closed the door. I faced her trailer, just in case she came blazing through ready for a fight. Zachary opened the door and Rane followed him as he approached me. He motioned for her to sit across the table. She shrugged and thumped onto the bench. I lost my appetite.

"Rane, this is Lauren." Zachary stood at the edge of the table between us.

"Nice to meet you," I said.

Rane waved. A limp, I-can't-believe-he's-making-me-do-this wave.

"Lauren was handpicked to be the Serving Arts Consultant on this venture." Zachary went on to list impressive credentials that I had never heard.

"I'll try my best," I said. I pushed the toast aside.

Rane smirked and rolled her cell phone in her hands.

"You need to listen to her. That's why she's here," Zachary said. "She's one of the best."

"Fine," Rane said.

Zachary sat next to Rane and nudged her. "Lauren's working with Molly Ringwald next."

Rane straightened in her seat and looked at Zach. "Really?"

He nodded. "Just got word this morning."

I looked at Zachary who then kicked me under the table. I did my best not to yelp. At least he didn't nudge me in the arm or pat my back, then I'd really hurt. Rane picked up her cell phone and studied its face.

"Right," I said.

Rane pushed a few buttons and then looked at me. "What movie?"

Zachary replied, "It's totally new. One of John Hughes' pet projects. He's the one who asked for Lauren."

"What?" I asked. Zachary glared at me. "I mean, right. That's right. We just found out this morning."

Rane looked at both of us and raised her eyebrow.

"I'm looking forward to working with you," I began. "I figured we could—"

"How come I never heard of this?" Rane asked. "Mom and Johnny are tight. I would have heard about this months before you."

"I'm telling you," Zachary said. "Super. Secret. Your mom might not even know."

"Whatever. I gotta jet." She hopped up from the bench and called over her shoulder. "Been real." She flipped open her phone and disappeared into a trailer.

"That went well," Zachary said.

"Really?"

"For Rane, that was an apology. Okay, enough fun stuff. Time to work. Do me a favor and help out Joe with setting up a shot. Samantha from Prod had an emergency and got called off set, otherwise I'd ask her to do it. It's super-simple. I was coming to get you when all that crap with Queenie went down. This won't take long."

I returned to the diner, the building fresh with new flooring, the walls painted, the jumble of wires and boxes and stuff had been hidden in corners and walls. Joe crouched in front of a black box with tons of knobs. He cupped the earpiece of oversized headphones and nodded. I tapped his shoulder and he pointed to a spot a few feet away.

"There," he said. Joe was the head of lighting or something like that. I took my place and he fiddled with the fixtures. He flashed the lights on and then off and then dimmed. I covered my eyes and he grunted. With a bit of effort, I put my hands back down.

Jonathan entered from the front of the diner and walked toward us. Zachary had mentioned Jonathan wouldn't be here until Thursday. Today was Tuesday. I fumbled with the sash on my dress, twirling it between my fingers. The closer he came, the faster I slipped the fabric from my pinky to ring to middle to pointer to thumb and back. Joe grunted and motioned for me to move to the left. When I didn't respond, he moved from his spot, placed his hands on my shoulders and put me where he wanted me to be and then returned to what he had been doing.

"Sorry," I said.

Joe nodded.

As Jonathan stepped closer, one knee didn't bend as much as the other, making his walk look lopsided. My fingers' pace slowed as I observed his change in stride. He didn't walk the same as he did when we first met. His confidence was there but off-center, like he missed part of what made him Jonathan Pearce.

Zachary came from behind one of the cameras and rushed to him. They shook hands and talked. The crew continued on their way, indifferent to the new person on the set. One grip bumped into Jonathan and barely waved an apology. Jonathan narrowed his lips and looked snarly. I was surprised that no one responded to him being here. I guess they were used to seeing him around.

"Lauren," Joe called and waved to the left. "Hands down."

I moved to where I was asked and reluctantly put my hands to my sides. My fingers still fluttered in the twirling motion of before.

While Jonathan and Zachary talked, Jonathan's arms cut through the air, like the strength he once embodied had been replaced with a hardness. His movements became harsher and faster. Then his hands broke the air, cracked the space between them. In the middle of a sentence Jonathan looked at me. No. He looked through me, like I didn't exist. I had become another speck on the wall. Zachary glanced at me, his lips a fine line.

Jonathan must have told Zachary that he didn't want me there. My throat tightened and eyes blurred. I placed my hands against a table for support. Lightheaded, I gripped the folding table so hard it squeaked away from me. Zachary waved his hands in the air.

Maybe I shouldn't be there. Maybe I needed to leave. Why wouldn't Jonathan want me there? I thought he liked me. He said he needed me. I remembered him saying that.

"Lauren!" Joe yelled. His face red. "Go right!"

I couldn't stand there. I couldn't wait for Zachary to come over and grab me. I couldn't take that. I needed to hide somewhere. The bathroom. I needed to find a way out of there.

"I'll be right back," I said and excused myself.

Joe took his head phones off. "Where are you going?" He called out.

Zachary made his way to me.

"I'll be right back." I followed the black and white checkers of the floor. I wanted to hide in a corner and get away from this nightmare.

"Dave can be such a pisser," Zachary said. "Like he doesn't know what Jonathan wants."

"Right. Dave," I said. Which way should I go? The bathroom or the front door?

"Unless it's an emergency, I'll need you in spot in a minute," Joe said to me.

Zachary slumped into a chair.

I could more easily get to the front door.

"Dave'll be ready for his shots in a second and we'll need you to spot for Rane's scenes with Jonathan," Joe said.

"Do we need to do this now?" I asked. If only I could make it to the door.

"What's your problem?" Zachary asked. "Dave is expensive. We don't want to waste his time." Jonathan approached as if saying his name made him materialize. I looked away from him. Everything blurred as I tried not to cry. I couldn't look at him. I couldn't stand to see the confirmation that he didn't want me there. I grabbed my bag and took one big step closer to the door.

"Zach. Jonathan told me that he'd like indirect lighting for this scene here."

"I know Dave. It's been discussed with the director. I've got to go with what I've been told. What I told you is what the big guy told me." Zachary waved to the director's trailer. I started to edge away from them when Zachary must have sensed my motion. "I am so rude. Dave St. Martin, this is Lauren Scott. She'll be helping Rane with her performance. Lauren Scott, this is Dave St. Martin, Jonathan's body double."

If I could . . .

Body double? Body double. I finally looked at the man I swore was Jonathan to find a man who stood, looked, and moved like him but wasn't. After a beat, I smiled. "Nice to meet you," I said. Dave shook my hand and returned to his conversation with Zachary.

"Jonathan won't be happy," Dave said.

A body double.

"I say so," Zachary said.

"Well then. You got it." Their conversation continued but I only heard pieces of it. I was too busy trying to absorb all of this. I nodded my head when it seemed appropriate. I looked closer at

Dave and noted the extra lines that deepened and seared, his stark hand motion. How could I have thought he was Jonathan? No one, not even someone hired to be him, possessed Jonathan's glow.

"Ready?" Joe asked.

I took my place on set.

Joe told Dave where to move and then fiddled with the lighting and camera positions. Then Dave lounged in the middle of the set while snapshots were taken and lighting adjusted to get rid of shadows on his face and body. With tray in hand, I stood next to him. My arm seared from holding the serving tray in midair for so long. Joe motioned for me to move off set and then continued with Dave who waited in the doorway to help them get the perfect shot of where Jonathan would enter to see his co-star. Dave tried to imitate Jonathan's facial expressions. I almost laughed. He tried so hard but it still wasn't the same. Dave then finished his duties for the day by walking down the path in front of the Oaklyn Diner. First with his hands in his pockets, he ambled down the sidewalk. Then he strutted across the street. And then he ran as if he was trying to catch a taxi. In between each take, the makeup artist powdered his face to reduce the shine. An assistant waited on the side with a glass of mineral water for when he became parched.

Zachary and I observed from the sidelines. Zachary would whisper little tidbits along the way. "He's Jonathan's favorite double. It's like a ritual. The word is that Jonathan thinks if this guy is his body double then the film will be a success. If this guy isn't here, then poof." Zachary spritzed. "No Jonathan. No film. Nada."

"That can't be true," I said.

"Go find out how much he makes an hour. Then you'll believe me. This guy can demand damn near anything he wants. All because Jonathan loves him." Zachary placed his hand on the small of my back.

Dave demonstrated how Jonathan picks up a cup of coffee while standing in an aisle. A woman with wild curly blonde hair burst out of the bathroom. "Jonathan!"

She ran by me, tripped on wires, regained her balance and then continued on her pounce. Dave turned, saw her coming, and moved out of the way in time for her to fall head first into a booth. She finally stopped with her legs flailing like broken twigs.

"Who the hell let her in here?" Zachary asked. He hovered over the girl and pointed at her. No one responded. She raised her head high so I saw a bit of her face. Her eyes dazed, a frown crossed her lips. She lifted up by her arms and shifted her body. She looked even more like a broken doll. "Jonathan?" she said to Dave.

"Sweetie, come with me." Zachary helped her up. He grabbed her upper arm, his fingers whitened.

She yanked her arm from his grip and lunged for Dave again. Within inches of his face, Dave caught hold of her shirt and pulled. "Hey!" she cried.

"That's enough," Dave said. She thrashed in his arms.

"Look at him," I said. "Just look at him." He's not the one.

Crewmembers came in closer. They formed a circle around the fan and the fill-in.

Zachary came up to her. "Look at him." Her face contorted while trying to be freed, then softened when she saw Dave's face. Her body returned to the flaccid state of a broken figurine.

From the front door came a security guard. "That's enough," he said to her. His hold replaced Dave's on her shirt. He put her hands behind her back. She slouched as she was led outside.

"These fans kill me sometimes. You'd think she could tell the difference between a star and his double," Zachary said. "All right. Get back to it." He called over the crowd. The small group that had gathered slowly disbanded.

"You okay?" Zachary approached Dave as he straightened his shirtsleeve.

"Fine," Dave replied. "This is typical."

Outside, the security guard guided the girl away. Her face bright red and covered in tears. She fanned her hands across her face, as if this would keep away curious eyes. I wondered if she would be okay. The security car drove away. The crowd separated to let it by.

Joe put the last light in place and took a test shot. Zachary turned to me. "It's time. Queenie looks like she's 'recomposed.' I'll go get her."

"I still don't know what you want me to do." After my encounter with her, I didn't want the job. I'd much rather help Lena out in the catering truck than try to show Rane how to serve.

"We're going to film with Rane doing it the way she *thinks* it should be done. Then, I want you to *gently* guide her to the correct way of doing it."

I sighed and tried to figure a way out of this. He looked at me like I had said something naïve. "You have no idea." I watched as Dave settled in to a spot. I tried to imagine what it was like to be him. What it was like to spend his life pretending to be someone else and never actually living it.

Near the swarm, Zachary disappeared out the door. Through the glass I saw him reappear in front of Rane's trailer. She answered with a handkerchief in hand. She patted her neck. Zachary's hands formed a steeple, his face intense, and then he got this puppy dog look, the kind little kids use when they try to get their way. She smiled and imitated him. For a second he looked annoyed but I don't think she saw because she went back inside and then reappeared dressed like a 1950s waitress.

Dianne, the woman playing opposite Jonathan, exited her silver trailer dressed in a tailored suit and a fitted French cuff dress shirt.

The brown suit pants and pale sky-blue top accentuated her strawberry blonde hair. She wore horn-rimmed glasses and her hair had been loosely pulled up in a bun. Her eyes sparkled. Her porcelain skin was highlighted with golden freckles that played atop prominent cheekbones.

"Hi Markus. It's good to see you again," she said through full but not puffy lips. As she moved through the crowd, she seemed to float, her motion fluid. "How are the kids? Good? Good." She walked up the steps to the diner. She waved at people as she walked through. I read the script for the zillionth time. I started acting in my expert role. After our first encounter Rane hadn't talked to me. I'm not even sure she was on the set at all. The first scene involved Dianne and Rane.

"You." Dianne approached me. "You must be Lauren. I have heard wonders about you." Wonders? I only read a script and ate toast. "I spoke to Mrs. P. Great woman. Very fun. She told me how invaluable you are." She reached out and shook my hand. "We are going to have a lot of fun. Don't you think?"

I closed the book. "Yes. I mean, absolutely," I said.

I had watched her films since she was a teenager and she played Jean in *Fourteen Candles* opposite Eric Stoltz. A film about a guy (Eric) who danced with this girl (not Dianne, I think the actress was Bella Cantra) and Dianne wanted to be the girl. Something like that. She had been in a dozen or more movies since then. One of the rare Hollywood starlets with a body. I mean, she's not supernaturally thin. I was surprised that even in person, she was shapely.

Zachary entered the diner and spoke to some of the crew. Last minute changes, I'm sure. Something always changed. I learned this in my brief time working with these folks. In the mornings, Zachary appeared from one of the trailers with a stack of notes. Usually the trailer belonging to Dan Folksmore, the director. Zachary made his way from building to building, room to room, and found whomever he needed. He told them the correction and then moved on. Then off they went to change whatever it was. Much of the morning was spent performing rework. When Zachary came in, Dianne waved at him. After he gave one last bit of advice to a grip, he approached her.

"Dianne. Great to see you." He pecked her on the cheek.

"Zachary. Are you ready for me?" She returned with an air kiss. Their fingertips barely touched so they were far enough away not to invade each other's personal space.

"I'm always ready for you." Zachary guided her to the corner booth. The director decided this was the perfect spot for her scenes with Jonathan. Dianne entered it and crossed her long legs.

"I'm so happy we're working together, Bill. How's Nancy?" She asked a sound tech. Next a man in a threadbare baseball cap and a worn Hawaiian shirt walked up to Dianne. The shirt gave away who he was—Dan Folksmore. He wore his signature clothes for good luck. He briefly said his hellos and then returned to a blue canvas tent outside the diner and sat in a metal folding chair behind a small black television monitor, then he put on a headset and eased back. All of this had been done in seconds.

Zachary pressed his hands against his earpiece. "People," he called out. "You know the drill." He looked at his watch and pointed at Rane. "It's time."

Rane eased down the asphalt road. Chin in the air, she strode across the grass in front of the building and sauntered up the cement path and into the diner. Without a glance at the crew, she took her place behind the counter, tray in hand. On top of it balanced a clear glass of water and silverware wrapped in napkins. Once in place, Rane's eyes remained on the objects. She stayed perfectly still.

"Places," Zachary said. Onlookers shuffled this way and that to stand, sit, stay in the correct spot. Once they were done, he declared, "action."

Rane smiled like someone stuck a prod into her back. She walked around the counter to Dianne. Water bounced from the glass onto the tray and drenched Rane's sleeve. The glass came crashing to the floor.

"Cut," Zachary said. "What was that?"

Rane looked at the ceiling. "I'm method acting. This waitress should be *really* nervous because of a new customer." I almost thought she believed it.

"No." He pressed the earpiece closer to his head. Zachary waved his finger and shuffled in her direction. "No. No method. Just get the glass of water and utensils to Dianne."

Dianne didn't acknowledge the display. Around us the crew waited in dimly lit pockets of the room. I felt like we were in the middle of a game of Simon Says and Simon didn't say go.

"But . . ." Rane placed the tray on the counter.

"No." Zachary looked straight into her eyes with the warning *if you mess with me I'll make your life hell.*

"But—"

"No. Dan'll make the call," he said in a low deep tone.

Rane opened her mouth like a baby bird waiting for Mama to give up some food and then abruptly shut her mouth. She straightened her clothes and got out of the way while an assistant cleaned up the shards of glass. Rane wiped the tray dry. "Fine," she said.

Zachary turned to the crew and called for places and then action. Rane lifted the plastic tray. It flew out of her hands and thumped on the floor.

"Cut," Zachary said. Dianne excused herself and headed to the bathroom. An assistant came from behind a camera with a new tray and a fresh glass of water and utensils. Rane glared at him.

"You need to clean this up," she said to the assistant who looked at Zachary for direction. Zachary shrugged.

The assistant took paper towels and shoved them across the pool of water.

"I don't clean. I act," Rane said.

Zachary muttered, "Barely."

"Excuse me?" Rane said to Zachary.

He flipped through his clipboard and then looked up at Rane. "I'm sorry?"

"I thought you said something to me."

"No, no. Must have been someone else."

Rane straightened her outfit again and returned to her spot.

I shifted from one foot to the other. The more she messed up the worse I felt for her. I hoped Jonathan would arrive soon. I wasn't sure when I was supposed to help Rane. I guessed Zachary would tell me when it was time.

Zachary sought Dianne. We had already lost time with the retakes and he wanted us to finish before sundown. He needed to find Dianne so we could begin. I was relieved when they came back, a sign that we were a little closer to the day being over.

They started filming and this time Rane drenched the table and spilled half of the water. She put the napkins and glasses on the table but when she talked to Dianne, Rane spilled the water into her lap. This time Rane's cheeks flushed.

"I am sorry. I don't understand the importance of the water on the table. How does this provide motivation? It seems pointless. Don't you agree?" She asked Dianne.

"I assume this is what a waitress would bring to a table. Perhaps I'm wrong," Dianne said. Her back stiffened. She excused herself and stepped away to change her clothes again.

Rane picked up her phone and dialed. Joe pointed out the sign that said no cell phones on the set, but she turned her back on him and continued her call. Zachary eased next to me and whispered, "I can't stand it. Give her some tips so she will quit giving Dianne a bath."

Behind the counter Rane complained into her cell phone. "Can you believe they have me doing manual labor?" She looked over and saw me. "Excuse me. I have to take care of something." She clicked her phone off. "You. I thought you were here to teach me how to be a waitress. What *kind* of *help* was this?" She pointed at the drenched table.

"I was told . . ." I began.

"I don't care what you were told. You're not doing your job."

"Then why don't we look at—" I reached for the serving tray.

"This is too much. They don't need an actress of my caliber for this role."

"Okay." I looked around to find Zachary. He was outside talking to Dan. The rest of the crew had scattered.

"They could have you do this," she said and smirked. She walked off set and headed for her chair and then picked up her purse and dug through it.

"I don't think that's a good idea." I wanted to get this over with.

"You're right," she said. "They need me. I'm one of the few players that brings some class to this place." She took out her compact and checked her makeup. "Who's going to clean that up?"

I took napkins and soaked up the mess. Anything to stop this conversation and calm her down. I've never been comfortable with yelling and I hated talking to her when she looked mad.

"No. That's not what I mean," she said. "You need to coach me on how to hold this damn thing."

I threw out the blob of napkins and returned to the table.

"You were supposed to try it on your own and then I'd help you." I looked up at her.

"What? Is this true?" She directed to Zachary. He had reentered the diner and walked up to us.

"Excuse me?" Zachary turned. He clearly was not in the mood for Rane.

"Did you tell this little genius here to let me do this on my own and then she would coach me?"

"Of course. We needed to see what you could do. For all I knew you could waitress. Like it was a recessed gene." He squinted. "Didn't your mom waitress? I would *think* you would have inherited that talent, since you inherited everything else."

"What the hell are you gaping at?" She yelled at a sound tech as he laid down cable. He looked around and then continued his work. I wondered if she would act this way around Jonathan. Would she be so brazen? I bet a single word from him would end it. I tried not to laugh, more from the discomfort of the situation than anything else. Zachary came up with the perfect responses and what could she do? He was the assistant to the director so she didn't want to make him mad.

"That's enough." Zachary returned. "Lauren, give her some tips. Rane, listen to her."

Rane hesitated. She looked at her phone and then looked at Zachary and then outside at Dan and then at her phone again. "Fine. You." She pointed at me. "How do I hold this damn thing?"

I showed her the easiest way to hold the tray without spilling the water. Dianne talked to Zachary. "I think we'll return to Connecticut. I miss Martha's."

"I agree," Zachary said. "I loved Connecticut. Very nice. We may vacation there sometime, especially in the fall." Zachary stopped in mid-thought and held the headset to his ear.

"Right, right." He looked over at us. "Yes. They're done. Let's go people! Places!" He waved his hands. Once everyone was ready he called action.

Rane picked up the tray and balanced it on her right hand, weaved her way to Dianne's booth without spilling a drop, well, if I didn't count the water that landed on the tray.

"May I take your order?" Rane asked. I was so happy, I could have jumped. Zachary clutched his clipboard.

"Yes. I'd like . . ." Dianne began. So did Rane. She mouthed Dianne's lines as if they were her own. Zachary's hands turned stark white, he held the clipboard so tightly.

"Cut!" Zachary called out. He listened into his earpiece. "Right. Right. Yes. I agree. I'll take care of it." He locked eyes with Rane. Immobile, she waited. I was watching a train wreck and there was nothing I could do. Zachary came nose to nose with Rane. "What. Was. That."

"I just . . ." she began. "Sorry." Rane's eyes jumped from Zachary to the floor to the ceiling and back. I wanted to hide for her. Get her out of the situation.

"Right. Sorry. Two. I get to three and . . ." He held his fingers before her, so close that I doubted she saw them. I wondered what those two fingers would do next. Zachary continued, "Can you do it this time without saying Dianne's lines?"

"Yes," she said.

"Good." He breathed deeply, stepped one foot away from her and called. "Places."

With that one word, assistants ran away, extras took their spots, sound guys turned knobs and readjusted their headsets.

"Are you okay?" I asked Rane. She looked vacant after Zachary finished. With my simple question her face turned to ice.

"And why do you care?" she said.

"Right." I looked down at the floor. She had reminded me of who I was and why I was there. I was there because Mr. and Mrs. P had asked Jonathan to look out for me and Jonathan insisted that the diner be used as an on location spot. I was there because the production company probably had a contractual agreement that they had to have a certain number of locals hired for this job. I wasn't there because Rane really needed help,

Dianne thought I was wonderful, or Zachary thought I was fantastic.

From the doorway, a familiar puffed blonde head of hair came into the room. "What's this? What are you up to, my Lauren?" Mrs. P asked.

"This's Rane. She's playing a waitress," I said.

Rane ignored us.

"What's wrong with her? You look tired." Mrs. P plopped into the chair next to me. Her neon pink nails matched her jersey t-shirt dress. The scent of Chanel No. 5 wafted from her.

"You could say that." While we talked, silverware crashed onto the linoleum floor. I turned to find Dianne covered in utensils, Rane nearby.

"What're you doing, Rane?" Zachary asked, his voice became the darkened voice that warned of storms and anger. The crew stopped filming.

Rane's gaze stayed indifferent. "I think my real problem is motivation. I cannot seem to connect with this 'waitress' character," Rane said. "I feel more of a connection to Jannit."

"Wait." Zachary turned away and spoke into his headset. "You need to talk to her."

Within seconds, Dan appeared. "What do you need?" he asked. Rane repeated what she had told Zachary. "You mean you feel more of a connection to Dianne's character," Dan said. He lifted his baseball cap and wiped his hand through his thinning brown hair. "Take five. Rane, come with me." He led her to a darkened corner of the diner. Dan grabbed a cell phone from a passing assistant. The lights glowed from the phone and made his expression haunting. He handed Rane the phone. In the light, her face turned red. She placed it next to her ear, the shadows fell on both of them. At that point I was quite happy to be on the other side of the place. Without looking up, she propelled the phone and hit Dan in the shoulder. Before he responded, she ran through the restaurant, down the steps, across the path and slammed her trailer door shut. Dan retrieved the phone, rubbed his shoulder and gave the phone back to the assistant.

"You. Wait here." Zachary said to me. He raced over to Dan. I couldn't keep my eyes from Rane's door. I wanted to see her and make sure she wasn't too upset.

Across the room, Dan and Zachary had an animated conversation. Zachary's arms flew around and he pointed in the direction of Rane's trailer. Dan stood stoically. Rane dressed in street clothes, her hair in a ponytail, vanished down the street.

Mrs. P and I watched her run away. "What is up with that young lady? They tried to help her and she leaves?" Mrs. P said. By the time Zachary returned, Rane had been gone for at least twenty minutes.

"Have you seen Rane?" he asked.

"She's gone." Mrs. P told him.

"Excuse me?" He asked. "What do you mean she's gone?"

"She left. She went into her trailer. She walked out of the trailer. She walked away. That's it." Mrs. P picked off each action with one of her long glowing fingernails.

"Hold on." He clicked a little black box on his belt and talked into the microphone. He turned away from us, while looking over his shoulder at me. "Right, right. Yes. I know she doesn't have any acting experience but so what? We need a waitress not a damned actress." He huffed. "Yes, yes. I'll make sure she's acceptable. What? Why? Why not? She won't be nearly as big a problem as Queenie. Uh huh. Right. Fine, I'll get someone on it now. Yes, I'll check on the problem."

I listened on. I hoped I hadn't been volunteered for what I thought. "It's all good. Right. Ciao. Miss Lauren," he said. I shivered. "What are your thoughts on being in a movie?"

"I don't—"

"You'll be wonderful," he said.

"It's not my—"

"Lauren. Hush. This is as it should be." Mrs. P held my hand and put me next to Zachary.

"But—" I started.

"You're perfect for the role," Zachary said.

"Don't I have to join the Screen Actors Guild?"

"I'll take care of that," Zachary said.

"What? I don't know how to act."

"Sure you do. You could do this in your sleep," Zachary said. "Plus this would save us a ton of time in filling the role. You would be doing me a *huge* favor."

Mrs. P whispered, "You can be closer to Jonathan."

Closer to Jonathan.

My next response jumped out in spite of my fear.

"I'll do it."

The studio costumer, Susanne—she told everyone to call her Reds—pressed and pulled Rane's costume. She had me stand on a block so I was one head above her. Reds wore citrus colors in a checkered pattern that reminded me of summer picnics and bebop music. A Rosie the Riveter tattoo peeked from underneath her shirt sleeve. Reds held the dress in front of me, her eyebrows twisted. Rane was at least four inches taller than me and four sizes smaller. I could barely fit the size zero waitressing uniform on my pinky. "Don't worry hunny. I make miracles. It's in the blood. My mama was the seamstress to Marilyn Monroe. It took a shoehorn to get her in that pink dress."

The trailer felt a hundred times smaller than it had the day before. Reds wrapped a measuring tape around me and then penciled down notes. She nodded, studied the numbers and then held the uniform in front of me. The nearer she came, the louder she snapped her bubble gum. The scent of Dubble Bubble wafted from her pores. She must constantly chew the stuff.

"How's it going?" Zachary poked his head in the doorway.

"We'll make it work," Reds said as she continued to study the measurements.

"Zach?" I called.

"Yes, Ms. Lauren." He took a step into the room. "I got two minutes."

"Never mind," I said and stepped down from the block.

Zachary came closer.

"Give." he said. The room became even smaller than before.

"Are you sure about this?"

"About what?"

I took a deep breath. "I have never acted and I know I'm not a movie star type and—"

Zachary came up and put his hand in mine. I watched Reds as she made notations on the table. "Look at me. You want to know the truth?"

I nodded.

"I knew Rane would quit. One thing I'm known for is always having a plan B. Is that right, Reds?"

"That's right," Reds said. She cracked her gum.

"Besides, you're a natural. The audience will love you the first time they see you." He gently kissed my cheek, smiled, and squeezed my hand. "Just like all men do." Zachary looked at his watch. "Sorry about this but I gotta run. Does that answer your question?"

"Yeah, sort of but . . ."

"You'll be fine." He rubbed my shoulder. "Reds. Take care of her."

She flung the measuring tape over her shoulder and put on a pincushion that had been fashioned into a wristband.

"You got it. Come over here. I got a few more things I need to figure out."

She measured a little more and went into the back of the trailer then came out with more options. Most I never tried on. She held the costume in front of me and then tossed it aside. "That's not it," she said. Or simply, "No." She took the seams out of Rane's dress and then put it back together. "I don't know why I agreed for her to have her own costumer make the outfit." With a sigh and a nod she said, "What do you usually wear to work?"

I described the uniform.

"Can you grab that and bring it to me?"

"I can run home and get it. Do you want to see it before I go on the set?"

"Of course I want to see it before you go on the set. What do you think this is, community theatre?" She snapped her gum. I stepped down from the stool, careful not to overturn the rows of outfits, rolls of fabric, and boxes of shoes, ties, pins, and jewelry. "I'll be back," I said, and then pushed on the hollow metal door which flung open with the slightest shove.

Mrs. P ambushed me as my foot hit the cement. "Seer was right again. We'll have to stop by and tell her."

"What are you talking about?"

"I'm talking about you being in the movie."

"Right. I'm fine. No need to go back there."

"Lauren, that's not polite. We must tell her."

"Okay. Right. Gotta go." I turned and sped toward my house. I didn't want to continue this conversation.

"Where are you going now?" She called after me.

I kept moving.

"Lauren, come see me when you get back," she called after me.

I didn't intend to be rude. I needed to get home and find my outfit. I didn't want to cause delays. I even passed Rich on my way to the house. He tried to wave me down but I was too fast for him. "I'll catch up with you later," I shouted. More delays meant more time between now and when I saw Jonathan. I kind of felt bad. I mean, Rich had been trying to talk to me for a while and his timing always seemed to be bad.

When I got home, I ran to the back room where I hung the laundry and plucked a uniform from its spot. I had washed and hung it the night before. It had been filthy from days of working. I passed Dad's room and noticed the bedroom door ajar. I don't know why I bothered opening it but I did. Inside my father was passed out, face down, on his bed. Peeking from underneath the bedcover was a bottle of Maker's Mark. At least he went for the better stuff instead of his standard, Mad Dog 20/20.

He lightly snored. I put him under the covers and picked up the bottle. As I closed his door, he called my name. I took a seat next to him. "I haven't seen you in a few days, Pumpkin." He hadn't called me that since I was little. His eyes watery, he looked at me like he did when I graduated from elementary school. "You know I'm proud of you, right?" He asked.

"I know."

His hand searched for mine and I took it. "Your mom would be so proud of you. I wish she could see our angel."

"Dad, are you okay?"

"You've grown up so fast," he said. "I swear you were just playing with Barbies and now you're so big." His voice nostalgic, I was afraid to pull away.

"What happened with the job? Why this?" I lifted the bottle just high enough so he could identify it. He looked away.

"I miss her so much. I never thought she'd be gone." I heard the tears in his voice.

"I miss her too. Do you want me to stay with you?"

He didn't answer immediately. In fact, I started to wonder if he had passed out again. I never knew when he'd get like this. Each time felt so random. He faced me, his cheeks wet. "No, you go." He patted my hand. "I'm going to sleep, I think." He smiled a tiny smile and then rolled over, clutching the pillow next to him. I put the covers around his shoulders and lightly kissed his head.

I didn't bother to check the mail or the answering machine. I needed to get back to the set pronto. I didn't look at the time. I hurried with the hope that I hadn't made Reds or Mrs. P too mad.

"What's this? Did you drag your butt through the mud? What happened to the stitching?" Reds flipped the dress around in her hands, pulled and prodded every inch. The dress had been through a lot but I didn't think it was that bad. "I'll call you when I need you. Don't worry hunny. We'll pull together somethin' perfect. Do me a favor." She chewed. "Let Zach know I'll be an hour or two? He gets itchy. If he wants this to look good then he'll wait."

Lena literally hung out of the truck. Her black t-shirt hovered under her belly button, her butt anchored her from falling onto her head. Her face bright from the blood flow. She must have been bored. Since the drama of Rane subsided, the crew went back to their regular jobs.

Lena flopped right side up when our eyes met. She held onto the edge of her shirt, which prevented it from flipping up. "Now what, chickie?" she asked.

"You wouldn't believe me." I knew the only reason Zachary asked me to do this role was because I had read the script, I witnessed the blocking, and I knew what they wanted. I told her of the most recent events.

"Believe me, they don't pick someone because the person's convenient. They saw something in you." Lena winked. "You know, this is exactly how some stars started."

"Nah. That's not for me. I'd be happy to be with Jonathan."

Lena straightened her back, nearly hit her head on the roof of the truck. "So you *are* one of those." She covered her mouth and then lifted her hand from her face and smirked. "I'm kidding. Don't get your panties in a bunch." She went into the back and returned with a cup of iced tea. "Here, so you don't think I look down on you for being a Jonathanite."

I took the glass from her and studied her face. "Jonathanite?" I drank some of the tea.

"You've never heard of that?" I shook my head no. I immediately regretted acknowledging her comment. "That's what we call groupies who follow Jonathan. The way they act, you'd think he was a god." She wiped her eyes with a napkin and caught her breath with each swipe.

"A groupie?" I looked at her.

"I wasn't serious," she said. "I don't think you're a groupie. The girl who jumped out of the bathroom is a Jonathanite."

"Right." I hid my face in the Styrofoam cup.

"You don't get out much, do you?"

What prompted that question? "What? Sure I do."

Lena crossed her arms. On the center of her shirt was an anarchy sign that had squished to look like a peace sign. "Yeah? Like when?"

In my head I counted all the times I had gone out. To come up with a short list I had to think back to middle school. I didn't think Lena would count a school trip to the Philadelphia Zoo or stopping into a club to use the bathroom.

"Well. No. Not really. I guess."

"We can change that. What are you doing tonight?"

"I—"

"You're going out with me. And maybe Zach."

Going out? I hadn't planned on going out. I hadn't done much since Dad had died. Come to think of it, I hadn't done much before he'd died. The most fun I had was when Julie lived four doors down. I hadn't seen her since she left. I wasn't ready to go out. "What if we run late today?" I asked. I still wasn't sure when Jonathan would return to the set. He hadn't been around in days.

"Whatever. Meet me here at ten tonight and dress like you're going to have fun."

What did her comment mean? What kind of fun? Going to the movies fun? Bowling fun? Or hanging out at a friend's house kind of fun?

"I'm not sure . . ."

"Oh stop," Lena interrupted. "We'll have a blast."

"Where are we going?"

"A club. You know. Dancing. Duh. Don't worry about where. I'll handle it." She folded the towel she used to clean.

I thought of my wardrobe and tried to imagine what to wear. I didn't come up with anything. "Lena? Isn't ten kind of late?"

"Late? That's early. The real party doesn't start until later. I haven't been out since we got here, which means it's been waayyyyyy too long." Lena swayed her hips like a belly dancer. No one seemed surprised by her dancing in the truck. I crunched on a piece of ice. The cold numbed the inside of my mouth. I was usually in bed around ten or at least busy watching movies. "Don't look so worried. We'll have a great time," she said.

"Lauren." Reds called from across the street. Her hand wrapped around the doorframe, her upper body visible through the opening. "Ready?"

I put my nearly empty glass on the counter. "Thanks for the tea."

"Remember. Tonight. Here. Ten," Lena said. I smiled and headed back to the trailer. I didn't want to think about tonight. I needed to stay focused on the day and week ahead of me.

Reds held what looked like a 1950s waitressing outfit from a drive-thru burger joint. What happened to my uniform?

"Now," she said. "This is the outfit. Go into the bathroom and try it on. I want to make sure it fits right."

It consisted of a bright blue skirt and white top with matching blue piping around the short sleeves and rounded collar. The skirt had plastic white buttons the size of Susan B. Anthony coins that lined down the center. The A-line skirt reached right below my knees and zipped at the side with a clear button at the waist. I expected to wear bobby socks and a pair of bright white tennis shoes. The size of a closet, the trailer bathroom held one mirror that lined the back wall. A dim bulb provided light. Even with the door closed, I felt like I revealed myself to this woman as I took off my street clothes and put on the costume. I meekly exited the bathroom. I looked around for her. Her back to me, she swiveled toward me at the sound of my footsteps.

"That looks great," she said. "Here." She held out a hat that looked like someone had folded a piece of paper, slit it down the middle and put some cheap clear fabric in the center. It was white with blue piping. Reds put it on my head and tilted it to the left. Then she handed me bobby socks and bright white tennis shoes.

"Turn," she ordered. I felt like she inspected me for my first day in the military. "Once we get you in hair and makeup this should be fine. Show Dan."

"This is what I'm going to wear?" I asked.

"Of course. It fits with the diner's theme. What's wrong?"

I held out the bobby socks and sneakers. "Isn't this a lot? I mean . . ."

She pushed pins back into the cushion on her wrist. "We can skip the bobby socks. Now show Dan."

"Yes. Thank you," I said and headed toward the tent. I advanced down the middle of the street, the same street I had spent my life walking to and from. The street where I had played hopscotch when I was a little girl. This street had led me to school and work. It had guided me from elementary school to middle school to high school. It saw me try to play hooky once or twice, unsuccessfully. It bore my footfalls the day my dad told me Mama had diabetes and watched me run from home the day I knew my dad was a drunk. Now this street looked on as I started something I had never imagined.

I approached the tent where Dan usually stayed while filming. The tent's front flaps folded open. Intermittently, someone walked in and then another walked out. I could see the back of his baseball cap as I entered.

"Dan? Reds told me to come over here so you can see this." I motioned to my clothes and then reached out to tap his shoulder. I caught the last of his talk.

"We've lost most of the day because of Rane. I shouldn't have promised her mother she could be in the movie."

"Dan?" I repeated. My hands trembled as I tried to get his attention. Maybe I hadn't earned the right to call him by his first name. Maybe I should call him by his last name or call him Mr. Director or Sir or something.

"What? Oh right. That should be fine." Before now he hadn't really looked at me. I mean, in the eye. "Are you comfortable with this? You look a little nervous."

Finally someone acknowledged that maybe I wasn't comfortable with the situation. As I saw it, I had two choices. I could respond that no, I didn't want to be in a movie viewed by millions of people around the world and I wanted to go home but at the same time I needed this, which meant I actually had only one answer.

"I'm fine. I might need some help, but that's all." The words floated from me like they were true.

"That won't be a problem. This crew has worked together for years. We're more than happy to help." He reached out to pat my shoulder. His hands were so large, his palm engulfed it. "Let Reds know this is fine and to send you to hair and makeup. I want to get some placement shots with you before we break for the day."

Chapter 8

A single lamp lit the barren street. The catering truck's door had been sealed and locked. Across the way the Oaklyn's sign had been turned off. The electric generator sat like an ogre next to the restaurant. A low humming came from it, like it slumbered. We had finished placement shots earlier in the day. Dan seemed happy with the results and no more drenched Dianne.

A red Chevy Cavalier turned the block, its engine sounded like a motorcycle. The lights flashed and blinded me. I covered my eyes against the sudden brightness. Madonna's "Vogue" blared through the car's open windows. *Let your body move to the music. Hey hey hey . . .*

The car stopped before me. Lena in the driver's side and Zachary in the passenger's seat. He turned down the volume.

"Hey! Need a lift?" Lena called out. Her bare arm rested against the doorframe. She wore a black top that dipped to her navel and dark blue jeans. A shimmering silver necklace hung from her neck with a bird in flight dangling from its end. "Cute outfit," Lena winked. Earlier she had helped me pick out clothes. "You'll need this," she had said and handed me what looked like a rumpled piece of jersey cloth. When I held it up, I realized it was a spaghetti strap dress. Unsure if this was the best outfit, I tried to convince her that black pants and a sweater would be even better choices. She scoffed and had me try the dress on in front of Reds. After some adjustments, Reds gave the outfit a thumbs up.

"Hey sweets," Zachary said as he got out of the car. "You look great. Front or backseat?" He asked.

"Back, please," I said.

He pushed the front seat forward and winked. I fumbled my way and yanked the front seat back. It fell into place with a clunk. The car stunk of cigarettes and newness. He got in and slammed the door shut then turned the radio back up. He flicked from the local club station to the rock station, the beat caused the car to vibrate. "Who doesn't love "Free Bird"?"

The concrete sped past. I hitched the dress lower toward my knees as it seemed to gravitate to my hips.

"Loosen up." Lena looked at me from the rear view mirror. "You're supposed to be having fun."

"I am," I said as I gazed out the window. I put my hands in my lap. "Where're we going?"

"You'll see."

"Here." Zachary handed me a rolled cigarette.

"No thanks."

"Just take a drag. It'll make you feel better."

I had never smoked and this stuff smelled funny. Sweet. "I don't think so," I said.

"If you take one drag then I'll leave you alone the rest of the night." Zachary pushed the cigarette at me. "It has to be a good one."

I took it from him and held it between my fingertips.

"What? You think you can get addicted from one toke? Please. Takes lots more than that." Lena changed the radio station. "Go on."

I looked at her and back at the cigarette, a soft burn on the tip. The ash grew longer. "Don't waste it," said Zachary. I lifted it to my lips, the paper stuck to my skin. I started to inhale when Zachary interrupted. "No. Deeper. Now hold it." I thought my lungs would burst. They burned as I held back a cough.

"Hold it," Lena said as she took the cigarette from me and took a drag.

"Let it go," Zachary said.

I went into a coughing spasm. My spit had dried up, my chest on fire. I thought I'd never stop coughing. Zachary reached back and patted my shoulder. "Are you all right?" he asked. I nodded that I'd be fine, even though my throat was raw. The coughing lessened and the room seemed lighter. Fluid. My body relaxed.

"That's better," Lena said.

Two blocks away, a box-like building lit the sky. Even from a distance the club throbbed with life. Beachball and volleyball courts spread across the front of the club. The ground was covered in sand. A volleyball appeared and then disappeared over the fence. Laughter and shouting came with each thump of the ball.

The Cavalier jumped over the curb and jerked me around the backseat. We slid into a parking spot, Lena waved off an attendant. "No thanks," she said and shut off the car. With quick motions, she pulled out the keys, flung her purse under the front seat and opened the car door. Zachary's movements were in tune with hers. I had problems getting out of the car. I got stuck halfway in and halfway out. My butt plopped on the doorframe.

"You okay, sweetie?" Zachary held out his hand and helped me up. I eased against the side of the car. I started to nod but everything moved with my head. Lena laughed. An echoing kind of laugh. "Whew. You are virginal. Maybe you shouldn't have taken such a big hit."

"That was definitely your first time." Her voice resonated in my head. She held my hand and led me to the building. "Don't worry. You'll be fine."

Numbed, I fumbled to the club. Zachary held me by my arm, which helped me stay steady. I had to purposefully think, left, right, left, right. It didn't help that I almost never wore heels. My ankles turned this way and that with each advance. When we reached the club, I sighed, happy to have the doorframe to lift me in. Inside the darkened building, I leaned against the wall, to help get my bearings. Little white flecks danced on my clothes like twinkling stars. I tried to brush them off but they multiplied.

"That's normal," Zachary said. He flicked off small drops of glowing white from his shirt. "They must be using black light in here."

The tips of my fingernails glowed.

Lena handed the bouncer her ID. His thick body plunked next to the door. His hair was hidden under a bandana covered in skulls and cross bones. He checked out her ID and then looked back at her. "I think I know you."

"I don't think so," she said. "I'm not from here." She danced in place, Nine Inch Nail's "Closer" leaked through the doorway.

"You were dancing at Club Risqué the other night. Aren't you Ttissy Tata?" He winked at her. Lena's face contorted as if her foot had been jammed under a five hundred pound weight. I started to move away from the wall; a little more at ease.

"No. I'm not Ttissy anything. The only name I have is on that driver's license."

"Sure it is." He squeezed her arm as he handed her the ID. Lena raised her hand and glared at him. He moved his hand to a lump underneath his shirt. She lowered her arm and walked away. I started to wonder if I should have stayed home. I wasn't sure this guy would let me in. I gave him an ID (not mine but close enough) but he barely glanced at my face. Instead, he spoke to my boobs. "Aren't you kinda young to be here?" I pulled at the dress's straps and hoped that somehow they would cover my breasts.

"I have to be twenty-one right?"

"When's your birthday?"

I told him but changed the year.

“Here.” He returned my ID. I held onto the doorway’s curtain. The room moved. In the distance I heard tearing.

“Oh no.” Lena pulled me next to her and wrapped my arm around hers. “No grabbing at curtains.”

A short pitch black entryway dropped us into a room that went on forever. Heads bobbed to the music. Arms flailed in the darkness. A sea of arms and legs jammed to the beat while others created music of their own. Some wore glowing sneakers and white clothes that danced by themselves.

“I’m getting a drink.” Lena grabbed my hand and forced her way through the crowd. I bumped into almost everyone we passed. I murmured apologies along the way. As we approached the back, I noticed that it was brighter than the rest of the bar; the area filled with multicolored lights that came from the ground. People’s faces lit from underneath like in scary movies about Dracula or Frankenstein, when the monsters’ faces glowed from what must have been a flashlight under their chins. But these folks moved, animated, alive. One man tilted his head back in a laugh with shadows shooting up from under his jaw. Lena pulled me next to her at the bar. She squeezed us between two guys holding bottles of light beer.

A long piece of thick leaded glass formed the bar. It had green, blue, yellow, orange and red lights emanating from underneath. The globes flashed and gyrated with the song’s bass line causing the bar to look like it throbbed to the music.

She balanced on one stiletto, lifted her butt into the air and waved down the bartender. The guys who stood next to us seemed to gravitate to her derriere.

“Hi,” someone said to Lena’s butt. “Hello? What’s your name?” He thought a butt had a name? I giggled. I sat on the closest stool as Lena ordered our drinks. My feet and hands tingled as I wiggled them.

She ignored him. I looked up to find a thin guy with a wide smile and a Beaver Cleaver haircut looking at me.

"I'm Steve. Wanna dance?"

I scanned the room for Zachary. He'd save me. But Zachary couldn't hear me. I waved at him, tried to get his attention but the only thing I accomplished was for Steve to look at me like I had lost my mind. Zachary continued to jam on the dance floor with a woman in equally tight dark clothing. I turned to find Lena doubled over the bar, talking to the bartender. I thought that maybe if I sat there and acted like a statue then the guy would go away. I stared at my feet.

"I said, do you want to dance?" He moved his fingers like legs pumping through the air.

Without wasting a second, he took my hand, turned and headed to the dance floor. I tried to edge my way through the crowd. How did anyone hang out at a dance club?

We reached the dance floor but he didn't wait for me. He moved to his own beat. His legs went one way and his arms went another. Even his head bounced around. My head swam with the sound and the scents of bodies moving in rhythm. Steve's cologne ignited with his sweat, the full smell of Drakkar.

Thump, thump-thump, pounded the bass line.

The sound deepened and reverberated in my chest as it drummed through my feet and into my legs. I felt the hollowness of my body with each beat. The room got hotter with every new person that moved to the music, crushed onto the dance floor.

I tried to match Steve's moves but I had a difficult time. When I swayed, he swooshed and when I bounced he ducked. Not to mention the fact that I felt like I moved in a weightless cloud. I decided to stick with the basic two-step. I swayed back and forth to the beat. More clubbers joined us. He seemed lost in his own world, his body moving to its own tune, his eyes closed. Then he looked at me and said something. It didn't matter. I smiled and nodded. Then he stopped trying to talk. I closed my eyes and felt the music float through me. The beat pounded into me. No words to the music. Only sound. Only rhythm.

I moved faster, my hands waved through the air. I reached higher and higher. I bounced with the bass line. My eyes closed, lights shone through my eyelids. The colors moved with the beat.

The music took me. I wasn't on the dance floor anymore. I floated and became a part of the sound. I opened my eyes to see Jonathan dancing. His body in tune with mine. *Yes*, I thought. I closed my eyes and moved closer to him. I felt his warmth, his strength. The beat became a part of me.

Our legs entwined. Our bodies moved together, closer, closer. The beat grew louder, more insistent, faster. He pressed harder. I wrapped my arms around him, pulled him closer. I reveled in it. In his movement. Like before. He pressed harder against me. Jabbed me. Painfully.

This isn't like him. He grabbed my butt and jammed me against him. The force caused me to cry out. I reminded myself that this was Jonathan. His hands wandered up my dress, the pressure not like before. I almost told him to stop. I waited for the pleasure to return. He forcefully grabbed at my breasts. "Jonathan?" I called out.

He didn't know, I thought. He didn't know that it hurt. I placed my hand over his, eased his grip. This was my Jonathan. The rhythm returned.

Someone pulled at me. I slapped it away. A distant voice called to me. I turned from it, not wanting to leave him. It insisted, yanked me away. "No!" I tried to cry, but nothing came out. I couldn't hear my own words. "No!" I tried again.

"Stop! I need him!" I screamed but it sounded like a whisper. Lost in the music. I staggered. Something pulled me away. My arm hurt from the force. I was led further away. And then the song, for only half a second stopped as I insisted, "*I need him.*"

I opened my eyes to find Lena's hand bound around my arm. The spaghetti strap of the dress had been ripped at the shoulder, half of it hung limply revealing my black lace bra and part of my chest. I scrambled to hide my bra with what remained of the dress. The fog lifted.

Lena fired at me. "You need him?" She pointed at Steve. Somehow we had gravitated to a dark corner of the club near the DJ booth. Steve stood before us and looked confused. I didn't understand. I didn't mean Steve. I almost said, "I need Jonathan." But the buzzing in my head stopped me from saying anything more.

"What's your problem?" he yelled at Lena. "She wanted it."

Lena released my arm. "Did you say? What did you say?" She raged at him. I fumbled to retie the strap. The music returned with an insistent beat. I tried to come up with an answer for Lena and Steve. "I didn't mean. I. No. Not him. I mean . . ."

"What did you mean?" Lena yelled at him. I tried to get between the two of them, not wanting a fight to break out.

I tried to answer for him. "He. He didn't mean anything." I couldn't look at him. I tried to talk Lena down. I tried to think of something that might appease her, at least long enough for Steve to get away. "Lena, it's fine. I'm fine. Let's leave." I nudged at her arm.

Steve mumbled something that might have included curse words and raced to the men's bathroom. Zachary returned. "What's up? Why so pissed?" he asked Lena.

"Did you see what that asshole tried to do to Lauren?"

Zachary looked at her blankly.

"Didn't you? Damn Zach. I knew you were self-centered but shit." She pulled out a hard pack of Marlboro Lights 100's.

"Wait. What happened?" Zachary asked.

"Can we leave?" I wanted to hide and get as far away from this place as possible.

"I'm ready. I got my number for the night." Zachary waved a piece of paper.

"After that? Where's the bouncer?" She lit the cigarette and searched the hallway and then the club.

"After what?" He asked.

Lena pointed to the bathroom. "Some jackass just tried to take advantage of Lauren."

"No. It's all right, Lena. He didn't mean any harm," I said. I inched my way to the door.

"What? You're going to let him get away with this? Have you lost your mind?"

Zachary headed for the bathroom.

"I just want to go home, that's all. No harm. I can fix the dress later."

Lena stopped and stared at me. She pulled on the cigarette and blew a cloud through the corner of her mouth. "Are you serious! Are you serious? Some guy tries to rape you and you don't do a damn thing about it."

"It's okay."

"Bullshit it's okay. Guys like *that* . . ." She pointed to the bathroom. "are the reason girls have trouble in clubs in the first place. How dare he try to rip off your dress. How dare he do that, Lauren?" She practically inhaled the rest of the cigarette. She threw it down and stomped it out with the heel of her stiletto.

Steve tossed open the bathroom door. "What's your problem?"

Zachary pushed him from behind. "You're my problem. She deserves an apology."

"Fuck you." Steve straightened his shirt.

“No. Fuck you.” Zachary swung Steve around and punched him in the face. Steve, not expecting the blow, jerked back and then stumbled.

The bouncer came over. “Ttissy, what’s going on?” he asked Lena.

“This asshole first tried to rip her dress off and is now picking a fight with my friend,” Lena said.

“Picking a fight?” The bouncer approached Steve and grabbed him by the wrists then bound them behind his back, kicked open the front door and kicked Steve in the butt. Steve fell to the ground, the door slammed behind him.

Chapter 9

"Lauren, I'm glad to see you." The voice I had heard a hundred times on television and in the movies came from behind me. His tone had been perfect.

Jonathan walked toward me. "I heard you'd be in this film." He put his hand on my upper back. "I wish we were together in more scenes."

Everyone else disappeared. Dressed in a pair of black slacks, an ironed button-down deep blue shirt and a three-quarter length tan leather coat, I nearly swooned when he touched me. His hair had been styled so loose curls formed little waves. I blushed with the thought of the other night, the image of Jonathan in the nightclub still fresh.

I tried to open my mouth but the memories were stuck in my throat and choked my words. I remained before him in my waitress costume and shuffled my feet. He looked confused like maybe he said something wrong or I didn't hear him.

The entire conversation became a lost cause since my brain had completely shut down. I played with a tablecloth, then I noticed that he watched what I did. If I said nothing I would ruin any chance of talking to him again. Finally I spoke.

"Yeah. It's a shame."

Although what I said was simple, I said something. I smiled like the Cheshire Cat in *Alice in Wonderland* and hoped that he found this endearing.

"Yes. Well. I hear we will shoot that scene tomorrow. I look forward to seeing you then." He touched my shoulder and grinned.

I could only compare how Jonathan acted around me to the way Mama described how Dad had behaved when they first met. Mama said he had been so charming and kind to her that when he touched her she felt like spun gold.

"Jonathan?" Zachary called. "I think you're due on the set soon." Zachary glanced at me and then at Jonathan. "You should really go over your script. Dan made a few changes."

"Thank you," Jonathan replied. I almost pulled Zachary aside to tell him that this wasn't the time.

In the same pose, I stood a bit longer to figure out my next move then I remembered that I was in the middle of doing something when he had called my name.

"Lauren," Zachary said, his hair touched up. The ultra-blonde George Michael style even more bright. Jonathan closed the door of his trailer. "We'll film your scene again tomorrow."

"That's fine," I replied. I only needed more time with Jonathan. That's all. Zachary turned to walk away. That's weird, I thought Jonathan had to be on the set.

"Why are we filming again?" I asked.

Zachary glanced at his clipboard. "Jonathan talked to the director and they agreed that it made more sense for you to be in the scene longer. That's all I know." He started to turn then stopped. "By the way, look out for Lena. She's still pissed about last night."

The entire ride home, Lena had barely spoken to me. She shut off the radio, even when Zachary tried to turn it on.

"I need silence," she had told us. I sat in the back. I tried to figure out what had happened. My actions must have been a direct result of the pot but I wasn't sure. I was afraid that my daydreams had blended into the night, which ensured I couldn't ignore them.

When they had dropped me off at my car, Zachary asked, "Are you sure you want to drive home? We can take you." I nodded still unable to tell them what had happened. Besides, what would I say? I danced with Jonathan? The entire situation was my fault?

"She'll get over it. Just look out for the whirlwind headed your way," Zachary said. "And if you need me, just buzz. I don't mind running interference." As he turned to leave, he said, "We should hang out more. With or without Lena." The last comment surprised me a little. I didn't think that Zachary even realized I was alive.

I couldn't do anything without thinking about the following day. I imagined Jonathan huddled in front of Dan's trailer as they discussed how to keep me on the set.

Zachary had given me the revised script, which contained more lines for me. I couldn't believe it. I floated down the lane and passed the seer's house. I wanted to leap into her waiting room and yell, *You were right!* Her small marble eyes looked at me through the large shop window. Her creepiness warded me away from her home.

I wandered back to the set. I needed to talk to somebody.

"You don't know me now?" Lena dressed in her standard jeans with blown out knees and a rock t-shirt. She rested in a folding chair outside the catering truck while she puffed on a Marlboro Light.

I stopped in mid-step and went to her. "I'm sorry," I said. Nothing else seemed appropriate.

She took another deep inhale and flicked the ash. "For what?" She exhaled.

"For causing all that trouble."

She raised an eyebrow. "I'm pissed about Mr. Hard-on. You. Well . . ." Lena brightened. "Next time some freak starts ripping your clothes off, you scream. Got it?"

I nodded.

"I don't need my friends being attacked on the dance floor. Besides, I missed a great chance to kick his butt." Lena got up and hugged me. I was relieved that she wasn't mad but guilty because I couldn't lie to her. I had spent much of my time with her. I helped her set up for the meals when I wasn't on set. We always had a great time together. It was like I had found a sister from another mother. So at this point, I couldn't hide the truth from her no matter how hard I tried.

"I need to tell you something." I said.

"Sure. By the way, next weekend we're going to Christine's on South Street. Wanna come?"

I looked at the ground and tried to think of what to tell her. A wormhole with ruffled edges lifted from the drying dirt. I wanted to follow the worm down into its chamber until the next rainfall. "I. I don't know—"

"Come on. One freako shouldn't scare you. I hear this place is the best." Lena smacked me on the back. "Get right back on the horse. You're going. This time, we'll go shopping before. Make sure you've got something good to wear."

How could I tell her? Maybe if I concentrated then I could shrink to the size of the worm.

"Good. This'll be fun. I get to play fairy godmother." She laughed.

"That's fine, I guess."

"What were you going to say?"

Chapter 10

Behind the fiberglass counter, I waited at my mark. I held the tray in the air and balanced dishes and saucers on it. I held it in my right hand and then my left hand. I walked around the counter to the booth. I served over the left shoulder, right shoulder, then back again. I held the tray in midair with it fully loaded to see how long before my arm would fall asleep.

"Lauren. I'm glad you are here." Dianne entered through the front door. She wore a deep coral dress with high heeled shoes the color of sand and a necklace to match. Her strawberry hair hung in waves and brushed her shoulders.

She eased onto a counter stool and crossed her legs. She put her elbows onto the counter and crossed her hands. She focused on her manicured fingertips, their white edges blunted. "All ready for our scene?" she asked.

"I hope so," I said. "I've read the script a zillion times and I've worked with Joe to find the best spots."

"Joe's great like that. He's always so helpful," she said.

"Yeah, he can be." I shifted the tray onto my other hand.

"If you don't mind, I can help you with the scenes. I know it can be intimidating. Is this your foray into movies?"

"Yea," I said.

"If there's any way I can help, let me know—although you seem to have been doing fine." She winked.

"Thanks," I said. I had no idea Dianne had been paying so close attention to me. I tried my best to stay out of the way.

"Have you seen Zachary? He came by my trailer a little bit ago."

"He said we'll start in a few minutes," I said.

Dianne looked at her watch. "Good. I hope this isn't inappropriate but I wanted to give you my sympathy. I heard about your father's troubles."

"Thanks," I whispered.

I placed the serving tray down, afraid the dishes would shatter onto the floor tile. My arms had suddenly grown weak.

Dianne placed her hand over mine and smiled. "Having an alcoholic parent is so difficult. I can only imagine what you're going through."

"Yup," I said. I pulled my hand away and straightened my costume. How did she know about my dad? I didn't think I had told anyone. I tried not to cry but my face grew hotter. "I'll be back." I coughed and ran to the bathroom. The door swung and thunked back and forth until the swaying stopped. Along the way to the bathroom, tears had streamed down my face. I was thankful that I had saved myself from crying in front of the crew.

By the time I got to the bathroom mirror and gripped the sides of the sink, the makeup artist's work had melted down my cheeks and streaked my neck. Black mascara rippled in little streams and stung my eyes. With each drop I thought, "That's enough. Stop." The more I tried to stop the more I cried. What had happened to my family? What had happened to the man who would take us out for ice cream and to play in the park? I missed the indescribables like how the house didn't feel so empty, how it wasn't quiet, and how I wasn't alone. Now he's almost always gone, even if he's physically in the house. The soul who raised me lost in his translucent eyes and frayed smile.

I covered my face in my hands and my legs came out from under me. I curled into a ball on the floor and hoped the pain would go away. Each tear shed brought another shade of numbness. I hadn't allowed myself to acknowledge my own pain, my own sorrows in so long that I didn't realize how much I hurt. I held my head in my hands. I wanted to hide from the harsh light of the bathroom. I wanted all of this to stop.

Someone put a blanket over me. A soft voice said, "It's fine. You'll be fine." My need to hide dissipated. I told myself that once I left this place everything would be fine. I rocked to help the pain go away and to make the crying stop. Finally, I shook off the last of the tears.

"Lauren. It's okay. You're allowed to cry. You'll be fine." The female voice came again, but this time it was in the room with me. I wiped at my puffy eyes, blurred from tears and makeup. Dianne rubbed my back through the blanket. Soft and reassuring she kneeled next to me. "You're allowed to cry." I held the edge of the blanket at my chest and clutched it tighter. I wiped my face on the fabric.

"I'm sorry," she said. "I should have waited to ask. My mother died a few years ago. She was in a similar situation." She crouched on the floor beside me. "I still remember those years leading up to it and how painful they were. I just wanted to see if you were okay."

I blankly looked at her. I didn't know how to respond. Should I smile? Nod my head?

"Look, I lost it on the set too. Mine was a bit more dramatic. I was in the middle of a love scene and started to bawl when I was supposed to cry out in passion. I had spent the entire night before cleaning up my mother after a rather elongated drinking spree. Let's just say the guy in the love scene wasn't too happy about my response. Hold on a sec." She got up and pulled a paper towel from the dispenser and rinsed it in the sink. She knelt next to me and wiped my face with the cool cloth. It felt so good. The once white towel came away with smears of makeup.

"Thanks," I choked.

"I thought the director was going to kill me." She sat cross-legged. "He didn't. He understood. He asked that I try not to do it again." She laughed. "He said I ruined a really good shot."

I smiled and she scrunched her nose. "Not the most glamorous of moments. And poor Eric, the other actor in the scene. He was totally freaked out."

I envisioned Eric's reaction when she started bawling on the set. He must have been horrified. I started to giggle at the absurdity of it. Small laughs, the kind covered by a hand or swallowed back and then she giggled too. And the giggles turned to laughter.

"The poor guy swore he didn't lay a hand on me. It took me ten minutes to calm him down so we could start shooting again." We sprawled on the bathroom floor and fell over each other with laughter.

"I heard he went into therapy afterwards," she sobbed.

"Are you two all right in there?" A man's hand waved as if calling a truce. "I saw you two fly in here so I thought I'd see what happened."

Jonathan poked his head into the room. Oh no. He couldn't see me like this. Lying on top of each other on the floor, our makeup ruined, clothes creased and covered in dirt.

"We're fine," Dianne said. She wiped her eyes with a cloth.

"Are you sure? You two look a mess." After looking around the room, he entered. I searched the floor for something to cover me up. To hide behind the small white tiles so he couldn't see me. I looked awful. I knew I did. I didn't need to look into a mirror to know it. I wiped my hands against the cold bumpy tiles. He offered us a hand.

"We're fine," she said and pressed her palm into mine. I pressed back.

"Are you sure you're fine?" Jonathan asked. He helped Dianne up and then me. His hand felt cozy and tender in mine. He didn't release it when he helped us get up off the floor. I wasn't sure if I should let go. I couldn't look away.

"I'm fine," I whispered.

"If you need anything, you just tell me, okay?" he said.

"Okay."

"Quit being Mr. Protective," Dianne said. "We're fine."

I nodded.

"I almost forgot . . . got word that we won't be in the scene together after all," Jonathan said to me.

"Oh." I wasn't sure how to take this. I looked forward to the scene. It was my one chance to be with him. "Are you sure?" I asked.

"They slashed some of the script and added other parts. One of the scenes that hit the floor was ours. It's a shame, I was looking forward to it." He smiled.

"Me too," I said.

He placed his hand on my lower back. I straightened with his touch. "Maybe we can grab lunch sometime," he said.

Dianne chimed in, "That's a great idea."

"Sure. That would be perfect," I said.

"You two should clean up. The makeup and costume folks are going to have words for both of you." He winked. "I'll see you two out there. I've spent more than enough time in a women's bathroom," he said and exited.

Dianne and I hurried to look like we hadn't spent God knows how long on a bathroom floor. We wiped our faces and scrubbed them with towels soaked in cold water then pulled and smoothed our clothes. Reds was going to throttle us. "Spin," Dianne said.

And I did and then she did the same and I nodded. No bit of grime had been missed.

"That'll do," she said as she smoothed my ponytail. "We have to make it to Reds' trailer and we'll be fine. Right." She made this statement as if saying *we will be fine.*

"Right." As we exited the bathroom a crowd broke. From the center of the melee came Zachary.

"Where were you? Jonathan asked where to find Dianne and before I moved he raced over to the women's bathroom."

"We are fine." I squeezed back. "Let's go."

The camera light flashed on, which signaled Dianne to become her character. She took her place at the booth. She focused before her. I approached, ready to say my line. Dianne looked at me.

"May I . . ." I coughed and cleared my throat.

Dianne looked away and then back at me again.

"May I ta—" I started to giggle. The image of Eric trying to explain to Freud the scene with Dianne stuck in my mind. I held my order pad in front of my face and coughed. I looked to the side of Dianne to help me regain my composure.

"May I take your order?"

"Why yes—" She looked at me and she started to giggle. The more she tried to suppress it the worse it became. First it was one giggle. Then two and then the giggles hit me. Dianne laughed at full volume. I held my breath to hold in the giggle fit. Her eyes grew wide as she covered her mouth and then hid her head under the table.

"Cut!" yelled Zachary. "What are you two doing?" His arms flailed.

"I'm sorry," I said. "I. I . . ." then Dianne and I made eye contact again. She tried to choke back a laugh and we both broke out again.

Dianne regained her composure first and then I followed. Zachary looked a little annoyed. I hyperventilated from laughing.

"I'm sorry, I'm sorry," Dianne sobbed. "It won't happen again." She didn't look at me. She focused on the utensils.

I sucked in a bit of air and swallowed. When we were silent he began again.

"Do you two think you can continue?"

We both nodded. I couldn't make eye contact with her. I returned to my place off camera and waited for the word "action."

No problem. I can handle this. No reason to start laughing again. Just stay focused. Stay focused.

"Action!"

"Hello. May I take your . . . your . . ." Dianne glanced at me and that's all it took. We broke into hysterics. I put the serving tray down before I dropped it.

"Cut!" And here came Zachary again. This time he approached Dianne. "What's going on? Why the . . . the . . ." He must have looked right at her because when I finished wiping a tear I found him doubled over in laughter, which of course meant that my giggles came back. By the time I stopped laughing I realized that everyone else had been laughing too.

Zachary held his headset closer to his ears. He listened intently and then had this look of horror. He choked down one more "ha" and said, "Right. No. I've got. Listen. No this is. Dan. Dan. It's fine. Really. It's handled." Then he gave me this look like "No this isn't *funny*." And yelled, "People. That's enough." Dianne stopped. Simply stopped laughing without a sigh or a giggle or catching her breath.

Zachary waited for silence and then began. "We don't have time for this. We need to finish this shot. No more." He pointed at us. "No. More." He pressed a button on his headset. "Have

Redsy come over here. And Anne from makeup. Dianne needs to be freshened up." He returned to his spot behind the cameras.

"Thank you, Zachary," Dianne said and then she gave me this look that let me know the fun had ended.

After the last take, I changed into my street clothes and found Mrs. P near the catering truck. Her hair was tied back in a red velvet ribbon. Her red jogging suit had a big white check mark over the right breast pocket. "Oh Lauren, you were wonderful! You'll be a big star now." She hugged me and handed me a soda.

"Thank you."

"I talked to that nice girl from the food truck. She said you had a tough morning."

I didn't want to talk about what had happened. I would rather talk about the sky—how blue it was or the seer—how bizarre she was, but not this.

"It's my fault." Mrs. P played with the tip of her can. "I told Dianne about your dad. I heard about her mother."

I cracked open the soda. Why did Mrs. P think she could do that? Dianne didn't need to know about my dad. "You shouldn't have done that," I said. I grimaced and slugged back the drink.

"What? Nothing wrong with it. She likes you."

"She didn't need to know about my dad. No one does." Mrs. P drank the last of her soda and put it in the fifty gallon plastic trashcan.

"Lauren. You overreact. It's fine. I apologized. Come. Let's go," she said. She picked up her purse from the bench. "We have work to do."

"I don't think I can go." I drank deeply from the sweet and tart cherry soda.

"We agreed."

"I need to wait for Jonathan." I wiped the sweat onto my jeans.

"He's waiting for you?" Mrs. P stopped and put her purse down.

"Well, no. Not exactly. He mentioned going to lunch and—"

"Then come on." She took out a compact and checked her eye makeup then pulled out a lipstick tube.

"Mrs. P, why do you do this? Why do we see Nuri?" I never felt comfortable with the visits.

She opened the tube and dabbed a little on her lower lip and then her upper lip. "Since when do you not want to see Nuri? We see her since you're fourteen. We always see her. She like family. Like your crazy old auntie."

I only went because . . . I'm not sure why I went. At fourteen years old, I did what I was told. Afterwards I tagged along with Mrs. P because I was curious. Nuri was mysterious and she seemed to have answers.

I threw my drink into the trashcan. "Fine." I guess Jonathan could wait. I hoped he could.

"Let me leave Jonathan a note so he knows I didn't ignore him."

"Go on. We don't want to be late." Mrs. P snapped the compact closed.

Drivers slowed their cars so they could read the temporary signs that warned them not to park this day or the day before. Police set up cones at each end of the street. Bill and a half dozen other guys busied with cameras and sound devices. Mrs. P and I waved from across the way while on our walk to Nuri's.

"Hey, Lauren." Bill waved as he checked on the sightline. He heaved a mobile camera onto his shoulder and strapped it on. The camera's size dwarfed his head.

"I wonder what they're filming," Mrs. P said. Bill tied up lighting, sound, and camera wires in a neat row and then taped them down. He then layered an area rug over top to keep people from tripping on them.

Moments later, we entered Nuri's. "You're back," she said with her thick European accent. She gazed from behind her clear ball.

Beside her, a steaming cup of pale liquid. Drawn heavy velvet curtains kept sunlight from entering the room. Jasmine and musk incense burned in the corners. Sconces filled with thick candles were ablaze with light. They lined the wall behind her.

Mrs. P pushed me through the doorway. "We need your guidance." Mrs. P kneeled into her chair. She put her purse on her lap.

I stood behind the chair. I didn't need to sit at the table. I needed to get the heck out of there. I wanted to return to the set and hang out with Jonathan. I should have been eating lunch with him.

"Lauren, you sit." Mrs. P called over her shoulder.

"I'm fine," I said. She glared at me. I sat down even though my obedience had a touch of *Is this really necessary?*

"You say Lauren big star." Nuri stirred her drink with a small silver spoon; the kind given to newborns. The spoon clinked against the steaming porcelain cup.

"I'm not a big star."

Mrs. P slapped me on the hand and kicked me under the table. I winced. Pain shot up my foot. "You said she'd meet the man she loves. How does she keep him?"

Why was she asking this when she kept me from having lunch with him?

"I could be having lunch with him now," I said.

"Shush," she said. "You have lunch with him anytime. This more important."

I folded my arms in my lap. Moments like these reminded me why Mr. P ran the business. Nuri silently pondered the crystal ball. She played with her teacup. I shook my right leg. She squinted. Unconsciously, I leaned into the crystal ball, trying to see what she saw but I only saw my own image upside down and disfigured. She gazed closer into the ball. Her nose practically touched the reflective glass. Nuri looked up and we sat upright and jumped back into place.

"You see?" she asked.

We shook our heads. "No, we don't see."

"You have met him," she said. "He is the one." Then she sat back and met my eyes. "You want to know how to keep him?"

"Yes, she wants to know how to keep him." Mrs. P responded with a sigh.

"Wait here." The old woman vanished behind a curtain of deep burgundy velvet.

"She will make it happen." Mrs. P patted me on the knee. "Not to worry." I didn't want to know what she searched for. Jonathan liked me and he wanted to talk to me. I didn't need whatever she had.

She whisked open the curtain and revealed a small blue tinted bottle. "Here." She handed me the bottle, which on closer inspection probably contained perfume when she first bought it. She pulled out a writing tablet from a pocket hidden in the folds of her dress.

"Say this," she scribbled on the pad. "You light a candle and you say these words three times before you drink." She pointed at the bottle. "This will give you what you want. Anything you want. Be sure you want it. If you don't want it, then don't do it." She accentuated each word with a slap of the table. "You. Must. Be. Sure. Or. You won't like it."

"She is sure. Thank you, Nuri." Mrs. P grabbed an envelope out of her bag.

The seer returned to the table and wiped her brow. "Open the curtain. I need sunlight and fresh air."

I put the bottle in my purse and with a swift pull of the coarse thick cord, the curtains flew open. Sunlight invaded the dimly lit space. As I adjusted my eyes I realized that the crowded street had been replaced with film crew. Directly in front of me, Dan Folksmore watched a monitor with Zachary at his side. I looked at them and then at the big "*Fortune Teller. Walk-Ins Welcome. $10 Initial Reading.*" sign that erupted with glowing letters. I tried to duck behind the curtain but I was too late. Zachary saw me and pointed.

"D-D-Do you have a b-backdoor?" I asked.

"No. No back door. Only the front." She motioned to the exit sign over the door that landed me in the middle of the filming. Mrs. P got up from the table and made her way outside.

"Hellllooooo . . . Good to see you here." She waved.

Dan Folksmore pulled off his headphones and yelled. "Cut."

"So good to see you here." She approached Dianne and Jonathan. I peeked through the doorway and saw Jonathan's expression. He seemed surprised. Dianne turned away.

"What are you doing here?" Jonathan asked.

"Lauren and I are visiting an old friend. Lauren. Come." Mrs. P called to me. I felt like a reprimanded puppy. Nuri returned to the back of the house, making it clear that she did not want me in her place of business anymore. "Lauren!" Mrs. P called again. I started toward the exit. The wooden floorboards creaked with each step.

"There she is. My Lauren," Mrs. P said.

"Hi," I said. Dianne's back was toward me.

"I thought you said this place was locked down?" Dan questioned Zachary. Dan lifted his baseball cap and swiped his hand through his hair.

"What? How did I know this place was open for business?" Zachary replied.

"You ask." Dan threw the headset onto the ground.

"I'm not screwing with her. She could put a hex on me or something." Zachary pointed at Nuri's sign. "You do it. I'll do plenty, but if you want me to risk finding out if this lady is for real then you got another thing coming." He walked away. Dan watched as Zachary left. Dan deeply inhaled then turned to the crew. "Take Five."

"Lauren," the director called. He looked like he had calmed down. He lifted his baseball cap and wiped his brow. "Anyone else in there?"

"Just Nuri," I said. He looked into the open doorway and then into the picture window to find the old woman back at her table. She sipped her cup of tea.

He whispered, "Is she real?"

A world renowned director asked me if a fortune-teller was real. Oh yeah, Nuri was real. She predicted the film crew would come to the diner and she predicted Jonathan and she said the diner would be crowded and famous. Other than that, she's a sham. I shrugged. "I don't know. I go with Mrs. P to keep her company but I don't know if she's real."

He entered the seer's home. The door clicked shut behind him.

Chapter 11

Few cars dotted the Acme parking lot. On an early Tuesday afternoon not many people picked up a head of lettuce.

Dan gave everyone the afternoon off, which was nice. We had filmed for ten straight days without a break. We kept going until we got the takes right, which usually meant we started around 9 a.m. and ended around 10 p.m. or later. As Zach put it, "We're on a schedule, people. Let's get to it." I didn't mind so much except for the days when I was dizzy from being tired. That kind of stunk.

The double doors swooshed open with a breeze of cool air. In the produce aisle someone in a brown shirt and pants sprayed the vegetables with a mist of water. The market seemed foreign. The aisles rearranged so baked goods had been moved to aisle eight and aisle ten now had the dairy section which used to be the deli. Even the deli guy was new.

I planned the week's meals as I placed each item in the metal cart. Spaghetti with meatballs and of course we needed to have salad. If we're going to have salad then croutons are essential. I could make Dad's favorite, fried chicken with mashed potatoes and green beans. I picked up a bunch of drum sticks, since those were his faves too. I planned on making the extra crispy fried chicken with corn flakes. He'd like that. And corn, cannot forget the canned corn. He complained when I didn't have canned corn in the house. He got cranky if I didn't have peanut butter, his midnight snack. Before leaving for the grocery store, I had stopped to ask Dad what he wanted. His room empty, I wasn't sure if he had even spent the night in our home. This wasn't necessarily unusual. His behavior was simply something I endured. I learned to wait at least forty-eight hours before calling the cops. The few times I had reported him missing, he wobbled into our home still half-drunk from the night before. His disheveled clothing, at times, spotted with the previous night's beverages. This meant I had to apologize to the police and spend the rest of the day cleaning up my dad. Therefore, I chose to go ahead and shop with the knowledge of his favorite things.

I wanted my favorite treats too, like the SpaghettiOs or Oreos and milk. Or a molasses ham and American deli cheese sandwich on Wonder bread.

I picked up a big tub of sour cream with the feeling of my father next to me and readied to tell him, *we should eat hamburger stroganoff this week. We haven't had that in a long time.* I turned to find an old lady reaching past me get a pint of whole milk. I jerked back, surprised by her and even more surprised by who wasn't there. I put back the tub and picked up the smallest container I could find.

The woman mumbled, "Excuse me" as she nudged by. I couldn't look at her. Freaked out from being lost in my own world, I wanted to apologize for being in the way but the words wouldn't come. I hurried down the aisle, eager to get out of the store. Lines formed like untangled ropes because only two registers were open. I took my place at the end of the line, like a frayed edge. I nudged forward as each customer paid and then carried away the brown paper bags or recyclable plastic. I bounced back and forth between the balls of my feet and my heels. I must have bounced too eagerly because I bumped into the person behind me.

"Sorry," I said and turned to find the old woman. I swear I caught her staring at me but then she looked away and picked up a magazine. I reached the cashier and put the peanut butter on the counter. The conveyor belt squeaked forward. I reached forward to put it back and started to tell the cashier the same. The woman placed her hand on my arm.

"You don't have to put it back." Her arthritic hand squeezed my arm. She tried to give me comfort but instead reminded me of the skeleton that lay underneath the skin. The knobby joints of her hands protruded from beneath the thin layers of flesh. The humanness of the gesture too much for me.

She patted my arm and then removed her hand. I wondered if she knew what I thought. "Thanks," I said.

I paid the cashier and moved away from the elderly woman as she arched over her cart. She placed each item with care to the conveyor belt.

I put the peanut butter jar on top of the last bag of groceries, deliberate not to shove it to the bottom of the bag. When I loaded my car, I placed the paper bag within my view on the passenger's seat.

I arrived home and lugged my bags into the house. I lined each bag on the kitchen table and then put the items in their new spots. I kept out the fudge ripple ice cream and scooped mounds of it into a yellow plastic bowl and then I spooned blobs of the peanut butter onto the side of the bowl. Even if my dad wasn't home, I could still indulge. I took my place in front of the television. Instead of buying expensive ice cream when I was little, we bought the generic vanilla and then spooned a dollop of something to make it special. We had Rice Krispies on top to add that extra crunch. On special occasions we would crush a Hershey's chocolate bar.

I turned on the set. I remembered that Jonathan's interview ran tonight. I hadn't even gotten into my Bug before Jonathan had finished talking to the interviewer. He headed in a rush to his car. By the time I had turned the key in the ignition, he had sped away.

"This is Jane Marogo with Jonathan Pearce," said the interviewer. "On the set of his latest film, *Jersey Diner*." The camera moved from the TV anchorwoman to Jonathan. "Jonathan, can you tell us about your latest endeavor?"

"Jane, it is about a man and a woman who rediscover each other throughout their lives. Each time they meet, they're inextricably attracted to one another but one of them is always taken."

"Really? I hear you're enjoying the magical chemistry you have with Dianne Lane. What's it like to be on the set with the most enticing woman in Hollywood today?"

"I'd have to agree, she is a very talented woman and I am honored to share the screen with her again."

The camera returned to Jane and settled on her face as she asked the next question. "Rumor has it that you found a romantic interest here in New Jersey." The moment she finished the sentence, the camera flipped to Jonathan. I turned up the volume, almost spilling the bowl of melting ice cream.

"I'd rather not comment at this time. If you will excuse me." Jonathan politely grinned and walked out of the camera's range. Jane Marogo called after him, "I hear she's someone local."

He continued to walk away. Jane's camera zoomed in on him. "Rumor has it that she's so special you arranged for her to be in the film. Jonathan. Jonathan. Does this mean the interview is over?" Her back to the camera, she watched him leave, then she faced me again.

"You heard it here. Something is going on with Mr. Pearce. If we hear wedding bells in the near future, they may be coming from around the block." She winked at me. "This is Jane Marogo reporting for Channel One."

Chapter 12

Someone knocked at my door. I had taped the interview with Jonathan and replayed it, just to be sure I didn't miss anything. I went back and watched some of his older interviews and movies until early in the morning. I had devoured ice cream, its remnants crumpled and emptied in the trashcan. After the evening's events, my house had been littered with magazines and photos.

"I'm coming." I ran to the door. I slipped on pages from the previous day's paper and grabbed the doorknob to regain my balance. I shoved the newspapers under the couch and into drawers and then opened the door to find Mrs. P.

"I came right from my home. I made you special donuts." She gave me a cup of black coffee.

I closed the door behind her. "What?"

"We need to be at the diner now." She placed a white bag on the kitchen table and started cleaning up the remaining magazines. "Why are you not answer your phone? I've been calling."

"It didn't ring," my head ached from lack of sleep. I thumped into a kitchen chair. I wasn't awake enough to sit gracefully. "I don't need to be on the set until this afternoon."

She handed me a glazed donut. "Here, this will get you going."

I wondered if the donut would melt into my hand so I'd have a sugary glop coating my fingers. "Wait, you said 'we.' Are you going too?"

Mrs. P didn't need to go to the filming, as far as I knew. Her visits usually involved socializing. Mrs. P getting up this early didn't make sense.

She hunted around the kitchen and living room. "Ah-ha! Your phone was off the hook." She put the receiver back in place.

I must have knocked it over last night. "Sorry," I said.

She sat in the chair across from me and bit into a cream donut. "I promised my husband I'd come to the set. Besides, the crew's leaving today. That's why I called. So we go to the set together."

What? "Leave? They aren't leaving today. They have another week." I wasn't ready yet.

She took another bite. "They call last night."

I put the pastry down and wiped my hands. None of this made sense. "Zachary said he needed my help today."

"You go. Say goodbye. I'll make sure everything is okay."

"But, why?"

Mrs. P took the coffee from me and threw out the donut. "You shower. We go. You'll see."

Mrs. P and I walked to the diner. The crew had packed most of the outside lighting. They scurried to put the heavy equipment, wires, and lamps back into their proper trailers and trucks. What had been an explosion of wires, metal, and electronics had been stuffed back into big black boxes. "What's going on?" I stopped Joe the lighting guy.

He looked at me like I had lost my mind. "We're moving on to the next location."

"I thought they wanted to film more scenes?"

"Zachary called the crew last night and said to get ready to go. I got a lot to do . . ." And he ran off.

Mrs. P listened in. "Find that guy. Zach-something. He knows. I'll go check on my place."

I searched for Zachary in the usual places, like the director's trailer and Lena's truck but they were practically abandoned. Lena packed her stuff. A small table of chopped vegetables and prepackaged snacks were out front of the catering truck.

"What's going on?" I asked.

"I'm always the last to go, just in case anyone wants something." Her head disappeared into a refrigerator. When she popped back out she asked. "You didn't get the call?"

"No. I mean. Maybe?" The days and nights had started to run together.

"Zachary was supposed to call you last night."

"Why?"

"This happens all the time. The next location is available and they need to get there pronto. We had to cut this short. Anyway, according to Dan the Man, he doesn't need more shots here. He checked the footage last night and said we had enough." She wiped thc counter. "You look kind of green. How do you feel?" She handed me a napkin. "Don't feel bad about us not going out tomorrow night. We'll get together sometime soon. You can come out to California and visit. We'll have a blast."

I sat at the bench. The street was strewn with remnants of the makeshift city.

"I guess so."

"If you're worried about the money, don't. Zachary will make sure you get paid."

"I hoped I'd get paid before you left."

Lena laughed. "I wish. Zachary has to submit everything to the movie studio and then you'll get paid." She leaned against the truck's side. "He does have money he can get to pretty quickly. He could pay you from that."

I picked at my fingernails. "I guess that'll work."

"Lauren, stop playing. I know you wanted to see Jonathan. This has nothing to do with money." Blood rushed to my face. "Don't worry. We all knew you had a crush on him."

"No I didn't," I said.

"Whatever. If you want to keep in touch with him, then find his personal assistant. She's cool. She's still here."

"You mean he's not here?"

Lena pulled out a cigarette and lit it. "Like I said. Just about everyone is gone."

"Lauren." Zachary carried a cardboard box. "Oh thank God you are here. I thought I was stuck doing this myself."

He slammed the box down. "Where were you last night? I tried to call you. I swear, I thought you ran off." His normally spotless outfit showed signs of sweat stains.

"I ran errands but otherwise I was home."

"Zachary," Lena interrupted. "What number were you calling?"

"Like I'd get the number wrong." He pulled out a page and ran his finger down a list of names and numbers. "Here it is. Oh-nine-eight-seven. I called the right number."

". . . it's oh-nine-eight-eight," I said.

Lena choked on a laugh.

"Didn't matter, my phone was off the hook anyway," I said.

"Avoiding someone?" Zachary asked.

"No, it was an accident."

"I should pay closer attention when I'm doing this. Anyway, I need your help to get this paperwork in order." He closed the box. "We need to attach all the receipts to the correct forms. And I need to get this done before we leave."

"I can help. I mean, sure." I looked up and down the street.

"What are you looking for?" Zachary asked.

"She's looking for Jonathan's assistant," Lena replied.

"Ohhh," he said with an I-know-what-you-really-want tone.

"He asked me to keep in touch. He said he would leave me his information and we'd . . ."

"Right," Lena said.

What if I was wrong? "It doesn't matter," I said.

I huddled over the box and sorted through the coffee and tea stained papers, while the crew finished packing. Mrs. P stuck her head out of the door, talking to Joe as he carried large heavy objects. She walked with him as he continued his duties. After what felt like an eternity and enough paperwork to reach the moon, I finished going through the receipts.

I trudged down the street that only hours before had been filled with chaotic activity. I pushed open the glass door to the Oaklyn Diner and found it to be sparkling and crisp with fresh paint. Mrs. P came over to me. The production crew had almost finished returning the Oaklyn to its original state, except for the wall color.

"I like it." She admired the paint. "I told them not to change it back." In the corner, Jonathan's assistant spoke on the phone. She looked like a throwback from the 1940s. She wore a long skirt with a long sleeved shirt and her hair pulled away from her face.

"Right. You bet. No. Of course I'm leaving. I'll be there in a few hours. Yes, I do." Her voice softened with the last words. "Soon." She purred and hung up the phone. "May I help you?"

"I was told to ask you . . ." I approached her but hesitated to get too close.

"What?" She nudged her wire-framed glasses up her nose.

I looked at Mrs. P for guidance. She nodded as if silently telling me to speak to the assistant. "I talked to Jonathan yesterday and he said he would like to . . ."

"Uh-huh." She looked at me like she tried to figure out if I made this up.

"I was . . . You know what. Never mind. It's not a big deal." I turned to walk away. I could find another way to get his information. I didn't need her help.

"Look," she called from behind. "If you want to keep in touch with Jonathan then you can write to the studio. Here." She handed me a card with the movie studio's address. "Just put 'In care of Jonathan Pearce' and it will get to him. He tries to answer his mail pretty quickly. Put a star on the envelope's corner and I'll know it's from you."

"Thanks." I read the card a few times as if reading the address would make it more real.

"Got to go. I'm going to be late for my plane." She nudged past me and raced out the door. She dragged a worn black briefcase behind her.

Mrs. P howled. "You see, Nuri's right again. She knows. She knows." She wagged her finger.

"I guess." I didn't think Nuri was right.

"Now you'll write to him and you'll become good friends. Very good friends. Jus' like Mr. P and me before we married. We wrote, we met, we fell in love."

Chapter 13

The film crew left. The Ps were anxious to have everything back to normal. Well, Mr. P was. He entered the diner, hesitated at first and then scanned the room. Like a cat checking out a new space, he touched each pleather booth, plastic chair, Formica table and then found his way to the kitchen and into the storage room. He patted the cutting board.

"Nothing changed," I called after him.

He sighed. "Lauren. Where's my spatula?" He called from the back room.

"I'll get it."

I found him in the storage room. His butt in the air as he searched through crates.

"It's not here," he said.

"That's because it's here." I pulled his favorite spatula from a drawer, the same drawer he had left it in. I handed it to him and he twirled it with familiarity. He smiled as the metal glinted with each swoop.

"So," he said after he had checked on the one instrument and moved on to the tongs.

"So, what?" I asked.

"What happened?"

"Happened?" I felt like I was in a remake of a Martin and Lewis film.

"You know. The movie." He flung the whisk into the air and flipped it so it looped above him. The metal blurred. It created a rainbow as it hit the lamplight. As it descended he held his fingers out. The action called the cooking utensil and encouraged it to land on his fingertips.

"Didn't Mrs. P tell you?" I asked.

He sighed. "You know the missus. I want to hear what you say." Mr. P walked over to the grill and turned a knob. A burst of flames sounded with the knob's click.

"Fine. It was fine." I didn't know what he asked. I assumed he didn't want to know about the filming and if he did, then I thought Mrs. P told him. My mind drifted to the way Jonathan's face warmed when he saw me. How his fingers breezed against my skin. How I waited outside his trailer for what seemed like an eternity only to find that he had already left.

"What did they do?" He rested against the sink.

I snuck into his trailer once. Just once, to see, you know, what it was like. I wanted to find out how he lived when he was away from home. I shifted one foot in front of the other, careful not to make too much sound and disturb his room. I searched the trailer for each item that represented him like the opened John Grisham novel with dog-eared pages and the cluster of bright vitamin pills. The most recent *New York Times*, its pages neatly folded on the table. The rinsed coffee cup in the sink, the one with a chip near the handle. My hands sighed against the cabinet knobs, the pantry door, the walls.

I entered the back room and found his closet. The folding door squeaked in its track as I slid it open. I reached out and felt the strength of his shirts and breathed in his clean, musky scent. I rolled through his closet and let his clothes, those things that wrapped him day after day encircle me. I lay in his bed, my head and body under the spread. I stripped off my clothes so I could feel him. I rolled in the sheets. I enjoyed their softness.

I dressed and went into the miniature bathroom and brushed my hair with his comb and dreamed of how he must have done the same thing a thousand times before. How he would smile if he knew that we shared this one simple motion. How the static from the comb caused my hair to form a brown halo around me. I giggled when I looked in the mirror and thought of how funny he would think I looked. And how he would turn me around and hold me and tell me he loved me.

"Why are you smiling?" Mr. P asked.

"Nothing," I shook the memories. "They were fine. Nothing special."

"That's not what I hear."

"What did you hear?"

"I hear that you were in the movie."

"Oh." I had to take one thing with me. Something that would make the moments real; the moments with him. I fingered his comb, the sound of my thumb against its teeth vibrated. The plastic comfortable in my palm. It had probably traveled the world in his pocket. It had listened to conversations, heard his thoughts, knew his dreams. He wouldn't miss a single comb, one that had nuzzled close to his skin, in the warmth of his clothes. One he'd touched a thousand times before and had grazed his flesh. It felt cool but quickly warmed in my palm. It whispered through my hair and formed lines where the teeth had once been. I watched as it untangled the strands. In golden script on the corner of the comb were his initials. I put it in my pocket. I imagined I did it the same way Jonathan would have done.

"What's up?" Mr. P asked.

"Nothing." Everything felt strange like none of this had ever happened. "I was in the movie. Nothing special. Just a few lines."

"Oh," he said. I wiped down the kitchen counter with a rag. Felt the hardness of the comb against my leg. I thought of the letters I had written to Jonathan, to Lena, to Zachary and of the replies. Of Zachary's words that he missed me and he was surprised by how much. He wished we had spent more time together because everything in the movie business was such a whirlwind and when we hung out he had the most fun. Lena talked of a new venture and implied that I should head out there. Lena called to talk about her dreams. "You're like my little sister," she had said. "I love your innocence." Among the chatter, Jonathan still hadn't responded.

"Lauren!" Mrs. P called from the front. "Lauren!"

"You know the missus. You better answer." He turned the knobs on the grill, readied to return to our regular routine. He waved his hands over it like the motion made the grill heat up faster.

I went through the double doors and found Mrs. P with her arms full of paper bags. Outside, the trunk of her mint conditioned silver 1965 Pontiac LeMans Coupe Hardtop was open and full of groceries.

"I thought you went shopping for flavored syrup." I took an armload of packages.

"I decided to buy more food. I want to have plenty of good food for our customers." She glanced at me and grinned. "It's good to have Oaklyn back."

"Yeah, I guess it is." I pulled items from the bags and put them in their proper place. I wondered what Jonathan did that very moment. If he traveled on a plane and looked out over the world below.

Mrs. P grabbed the last bag and disappeared into the kitchen. This meant I finished the morning rituals. I opened the shades to find dozens of people with their bodies pressed against the glass. I wondered if they had been there the entire time.

I knocked on the pane to gain their attention. "I'm sorry," I said. "We're not open yet." I pointed to the clock on the wall, hoping they understood what I said. One man's eyes followed my fingers and nodded. He turned to the others and seemed to be explaining it to them. I returned to filling the sugar containers, sure the grains didn't spill all over the counter. I hated when that happened. It made everything so sticky. I always missed granules that melted into a syrupy glue. I looked at the clock one more time and then headed to the front door. The scent of the heated grill filled the room. The coffee machines percolated and brought the repetitive sound of water as it steamed through the grounds.

Out of the window, a trail of people slinked from the front door down the stairs and spilled into the street. I searched for the end and saw the line of multicolored clothes and shifting bodies turn the corner and continue down the path. I reluctantly opened the door.

They pressed their way past me, my body pinned between the door and the wall. "Excuse me," a man said as he made his way to the counter. Along with the bodies came their voices, the chatter of excitement. I forced my way from the wall. "Excuse me, excuse me . . ." I mumbled and nudged to the counter.

A person occupied every booth, every chair, every stool, every spot on the floor.

"Miss," a small woman with short auburn hair waved to get my attention.

"Yes?"

"Is this where Dianne sat?" She pointed at the booth closest to the front door. "I want to sit where Dianne sat."

I wanted to say, *You don't deserve to sit where Dianne sat. You don't deserve to be in the same space as her. You shouldn't have bothered to come here and act like you know someone like Dianne. Because you don't. You never will.* I fought the urge to say this and more.

"Sure," I said.

The woman grinned and sat, her hand fanned the pleather seat as if this would bring Dianne to her. I almost laughed.

Cameras clicked and the pages of autograph books flew open, pens pointed at me. Nameless voices asked, "Where were they?

How long were they here? What did they eat? Do you have pictures? Were they nice?"

My breath caught in my throat as they drew closer. They reached for me to ask a question or get an answer. I tried to get away from them. "What?" I asked. I backed into the counter, my fingers whitened with my grip. I closed my eyes.

"I'll answer your questions." Mrs. P's voice came from the kitchen. I opened my eyes to find her wave a towel through the breezeway. They edged to her, ripped away from me. The flashes dissipated.

I ran to the back office, slammed the door behind me. The small room brought back solace. I could hear them talking in the diner. I could hear questions thrown at Mrs. P. I closed my eyes and listened for them leaving.

I took the comb from my pocket and held it in my hands. I rubbed the teeth against my fingers. It hummed with the motion as it glided against my leg. It circled my inner thigh and along the curve of my hip. I gripped it to bring him back to me. The teeth cut into my palm. I held my breath for a moment to ease the ache, then with my exhale came a release. I opened my eyes and looked at the comb, imagined how Jonathan traveled with it. Imagined how intimately it had touched him. I placed it against my skin and skimmed my collarbone and my neck up into the strands of hair. I closed my eyes again to enjoy the sensation as it tickled each fiber.

"Lauren?" A knock on the door. I jammed the comb back into my pocket.

"Yeah?" I sounded distant like my voice tried to come back from another place, another time, another person.

"What are you doing in there? Are you okay?" It was Mr. P. The doorknob jerked.

"I'm sorry," I got up and unlocked the door. "Come in."

The door opened. "What happened?" He slid into the office and closed the door behind him. Sounds of the crowd invaded through the crack under the door.

"Nothing. I'm fine." I pulled my hair into a rubber band. My thick strands heavy against my neck.

"Are you sure?" He asked. "You didn't seem fine."

The murmurs lessened. Mrs. P must have told them what they wanted to hear.

"I just got freaked, that's all." I looked down at the desktop, avoiding eye contact.

He rested on the corner of the desk. "Yeah, well, I guess that's understandable."

We sat in silence for a moment. We listened to the world outside and enjoyed the quiet of the room.

"Mr. P?" Mrs. P had told me about how he had attended an auction after he met her and found the structure that became the Oaklyn Diner. Mrs. P said she had been surprised when the man she had dated only a few days gave it to her. She'd told me, "*Lauren*, you find a man who'll buy you a restaurant and you have found the *world*."

"Is it true?" I asked him.

"Is what true?"

"How you bought this place for Mrs. P. That this was your wedding present to her?"

He looked at the floor and then looked at his shoes, his feet crossed before him. He smiled like he remembered a moment only one or two shared. "There are many truths, Lauren. And sometimes, the truth of now is better than the truth of then."

I wasn't sure what that meant but before I could ask he said, "I think Mrs. P handled those crazies. Let's get back to work."

"But what did—"

"Let's go." And then he got up and walked out of the office. The doorway opened to a restaurant full of people. They intently listened to Mrs. P as she spoke in the center of the diner. Mr. P weaved through the patrons and took his place next to his wife and kissed her cheek. She raised her hand and caressed his face without looking at him. As if this motion had been done a million times before.

Chapter 14

When Mrs. P called, she only said, "Lauren. Come here now." In the background trays crashed and voices elevated. Monica and Dotty were on duty but I guess things had gotten out of hand.

I threw on my uniform and ran to work because I was afraid that something was wrong. When I got there Mrs. P talked to a customer, started a fresh pot of coffee, rang someone up, and served a table. I had never seen her with a hair out of place, until then. She served the customers while her husband cooked. Dotty scurried from one table to another while Monica stayed at the register, the line grew by the second. Even though the crowds had died down over the last several weeks, the diner remained packed.

I checked in with Dotty to see how I could help. She directed me to grab orders piling up in the cubby. Customers quickly became annoyed due to the perceived lack of service. When the rush was over, we took a break at the counter before the next surge of hungry people.

Monica headed to the bathroom to freshen up while Dotty called her boyfriend. They had only started dating the week prior. Mrs. P looked at her reflection in the metal pitcher. She wiped off the sweat with a napkin and replaced hair strands with the tips of her fingers and then poured each of us a glass.

"This came for you." Mrs. P handed me a red envelope, postmarked from California. I tore it open. I could barely stand still.

Either this was a note from Jonathan (fingers crossed) or a letter from Lena. We had talked about me working for her but I always thought of it in a conceptual way.

"What do you think?" Mr. P behind his desk as he listened to my retelling of Lena's offer. A corner of his office had been dedicated to interview requests by newspapers and magazines, and then there was the fan mail. People wanted to know about the stars. Calls came in daily. They offered to interview us before the movie premiered.

"What you want to do?" Mr. P asked. I leaned against the doorway. I held my favorite mug while my fingers played with a chip near the handle.

"I'm not sure." I drank the bitter and sweet coffee. I had used a touch too little cream. Lena knew I wanted a change and she had talked about starting her own catering company so the letter wasn't a complete surprise. I suppose Lena wanted to make the offer official by putting it in writing. I knew what I hoped for. I knew what I needed. I had written to Jonathan many times. I knew he read them because he had promised to correspond. His lack of response meant that he silently agreed. I loved his stoicism in these moments. I didn't need for him to reply and tell me that we were in sync. Mr. P reached over and grabbed a handful of fan letters and opened them. "Some of these are just crazies. I don't answer those."

"What about the others?"

"I say the movie was great and the stars were great. That's it." He skimmed the pages.

"You weren't here." I sipped from the cup.

"They need to believe. I let them." He threw the letter into the trash.

"Believe in what?"

He shrugged. "Something. They need hope. I give hope by telling what they want to hear. Otherwise they wouldn't write." He pointed at Lena's note. "What do you think?"

"I don't know yet." In my chats with Lena I had mentioned how much fun it would be to live in California and how I had dreamed of a new life. I never thought she would respond with a job offer. I had always lived in New Jersey. I may have dreamed of moving away but I never thought I would.

"We'll miss you. If you leave." Mr. P's voice quieted. "We'll miss you."

"I'll miss you too." The thought of uprooting sank in. What did this mean? At first I couldn't stand still because I was so excited at the idea. I came to Mr. P since I figured if this was a bad idea then he would tell me.

"Lauren. The guy at table eight needs his check." Dotty called over. For some reason the Ps called me when they needed help with an emergency. I guess their need had spread to the new waitresses as well.

"Right. I'll be right there."

During my lunch break, I munched on a BLT. This time of year the Jersey tomatoes were juicy and meaty. Mr. P had a shipment of bacon that crisped up nicely when cooked high on the grill. I took another bite and continued writing a note to Jonathan.

"Lauren." Mrs. P came over with a glass pitcher of iced tea and refilled my glass.

"Thank you."

She pulled out a chair and sat down. The pitcher clinked when she placed it on the table. "You sure?" she asked.

"About what?" I had been writing about my plans to visit California and my potential move. I wanted his opinion since this meant we could see more of each other.

"I mean, you sure about him?" She tapped my notebook.

"Of course I'm sure." I continued writing. After Jonathan left, I had shared with Mrs. P that he wanted to see me and he tried to call me but I was never home. I told her about how he invited me to visit and that we wrote letters to each other every day.

"These stories, they . . ." She quieted. "Are you sure?" She asked again.

I couldn't get him out of my head. I wrote him letter after letter. I even sent him a care package. Nothing special, just keepsakes so he wouldn't forget me like photos from when he was on set. Ones of me and him together. I sent him strands of my hair because he had commented on how much he loved it. I hoped he didn't think that was weird. I brushed it with his comb so that I actually gave him a little bit of both of us in each curlycue. I knew he would come back. He had promised. I quit telling Mrs. P about him when she started acting like this.

"Isn't he great? I can't wait to see him again." I had collected his newspaper clippings and taped his interviews and shows. I wanted to see if he would talk to me again like he did the day Mr. Smarthey came to the diner.

"He called?"

"Of course he called. Why wouldn't he call?" I looked up from my writing. I knew he'd call the moment his schedule became less hectic. I never noticed the lines on her face and how her makeup seemed cracked. "You don't believe me?" I asked.

Mrs. P frowned. "It's just . . ."

I edged out of the seat, scooped up my plates and headed to the kitchen. "I have to check on my customers." I rinsed off my dishes and put them in the dishwasher and then returned to my tables.

If Mrs. P got close then I found a reason to go to another part of the diner. What was the big deal? Of course he'd return. Of course he wanted to see me. It didn't matter what she thought. All that mattered was I knew the truth.

Chapter 15

Not quite daylight but enough for streetlights to dim. Moments passed and a lone car eased by. The hum of its engine echoed and then another passed, this time Steve Perry sang, *Our love holds on, holds on . . .* The music lessened as the distance between me and the car increased. Lights blinked on and climbed from upstairs to downstairs. Inside homes alarm clocks beeped.

On the street corner of Lexington and Thirtieth Street, I found a standard blue metal box with a listing of when the parcels would be picked up. It never moved or waivered. Bolted to a cement block, it remained a constant throughout the years.

This morning, I stopped in front of it with the letters ready to send. The fancy envelopes with threads of fabric soft in my hands. My skin damp with the knowledge that the morning mist would turn to humid heat by noon. My mind blanked. Something inside me said *This is wrong.*

"Hi Lauren." Rich, wearing a bright white t-shirt, jeans, and workmen's boots called from across the street. I jumped when he spoke.

"Oh hi." I fumbled with the letters. I placed them behind my back and then on top of the mailbox.

"What are you doing? You've been standing there for a while."

Great. He had watched as I made an ass of myself and wished for a gust of wind to drop the letters inside the mail slot. "Nothing," I said. I wanted him to walk away. Please walk away. He didn't walk away. “Sending letters,” I said. I opened the slot and dropped them in. I heard them thunk when they hit the bottom.

“I was wondering if—” He looked to the left and then the right and crossed the street. The second he reached me I wanted to leave.

“Rich, I gotta run. I’m going to be late.” I looked at my watch and began to walk away.

“Oh right. I’ll walk with ya.” He hurried over and caught up with me. I tried to act like he wasn’t there. Once he was in step with me, he started again.

“Lauren. I wondered if—”

“Did you see that Jonathan Pearce movie on the late, late show last night?”

“No. I didn’t catch it. I was wondering if . . .”

“It was only the best movie he’s ever made. I’m sure when I see him next he’ll want to talk all about it.” I glanced at Rich.

“See him next?” he asked.

“Sure. When I get to California.” I looked ahead, anticipating the Oaklyn Diner to appear.

Rich’s steps slowed. “Are you like . . .”

“With him? Sorta. I mean. Yeah, you could say that, I guess.” Rich wasn’t next to me anymore. I looked back to find him in the middle of the walkway. “What’s wrong?” I asked.

“Nothing. I mean. I didn’t know.” He shifted his stance, put one hand in his pocket and the other motioned to me. “You’re *with* him?”

“I guess not technically with him but I will be. Why? What’s up?” I adjusted my backpack, its contents light. I hoped he wouldn’t ask more questions.

Rich looked up at the sky. “Look Lauren. I guess I don’t understand but if you are free do you want to go to the movies with me on Friday night?”

"Movies? Sure." I couldn't say no, but I needed to make sure he understood.

"Great!" He caught back up. The sound of his footfalls no longer hard against the cement. He seemed to barely touch the ground. We walked the rest of the way to the diner. I filled him in on the best parts of the movie.

He interrupted, "When we go out, are you going to talk about Jonathan the whole time?"

"Rich. You know we're going out as friends, right? I mean we can only be friends." This time he stopped.

A half block away was the diner. The Ps were already inside. I could see Monica through the window pane. She must have been prepping for the morning rush. Mrs. P wiped down tables. I returned to Rich.

"I wanted to be honest with you. We'll have a great time at the movies," I said.

Rich passed me, his steps thundered against the pavement.

"What about breakfast?" I called after him. He looked at the ground and then across the street. Mr. Lettice drove by and honked good morning. I waved. Exhaust billowed from the car's tailpipe.

"I'm late for work." Rich's voice trailed off as he turned the corner.

Chapter 16

Mornings brought the possibility that I would hear from him. I calculated how fast my mailings would take to get from my post office to the studios and then to him. I worried that Goliath, the movie studio, didn't forward my letters. So, I called.

"Hold please." The receiver filled with silence.

"Central mail." A man answered. I explained my situation. Jonathan and I were corresponding and I needed to be sure he received the letters.

"Lady, if you really wanted him to get the letters, why don't you send them to his house? You being a good friend and all?"

"I don't have his home address," I said. "He left before I had a chance to get it."

"You're out of luck." He hung up.

The bastard. I redialed the studio and asked for the mailroom again.

"Central mail."

"Look. I need to make sure he got those letters. If you give me his home address, I won't call anymore. I can resend the letters to his home," I said. I picked up my signed and framed photo of Jonathan. He had sent it to me after he returned to LA. One of my greatest treasures from our continued communications.

"What? Are you crazy? You keep calling and I'll call the cops." He hung up.

I looked at the receiver and held the frame against my chest. I redialed.

"Goliath Studios. May I direct your call?"

"Central mailroom, please."

"Thank you."

Silence.

I played with the curl of the phone cord. My foot bounced as I waited for the jerk to answer.

The line clicked open. "Central mail," he answered.

"Who the hell do you think you are? You prick! You're going to tell me what happened to my—"

Click.

I slammed the photograph against the table. The glass cracked. Damn it! The fucker hung up on me again. I redialed.

"Goliath Studios."

"Give me Central Mail." I paced. The phone cord stretched to its limit. It forced me to walk in the opposite direction.

"I'm sorry but no one is answering. Can you call back?"

"I'll do that." I slammed the phone down and found myself inches from the wall, wrapped in the cord. I unraveled from it and became angrier knowing *that* man sat next to the phone and laughed. What if that guy threw the letters out? He sounded like the type. That's a federal offense.

I picked up the phone and dialed Lena. "I'll do it. When do you need me there?"

"Are you serious?"

"Of course, I'm serious."

"This is going to be amazing! Don't worry, you can stay with me, at least until you find a place. No worries."

"Excellent."

"Did I tell you? I just landed a contract with one of the best produce suppliers in LA. I've been trying to work with them for months."

"That's fantastic," I said. I curled the phone cord around my fingers again and stared at the cracked photograph. The severe split between Jonathan and I would be repaired soon enough.

Chapter 17

I filled my keepsake box with everything I needed for the visit. I wasn't sure how to dress. I opted to wear a pair of black cotton pants and a blue long sleeved shirt. I usually saved this for Sunday Services. I had spent the morning prepping Dad. He had stabilized a little or at least more than he had in a while. One of his crew arranged for him to act as an alternate at a warehouse for whenever one of the long-term staff called out sick. This deal seemed to work well for dad. Not a lot of pressure. On days they needed an extra hand, he received a last minute phone call asking if he was available. If he felt up to it, he took the gig and was paid as soon as he finished the work. I was sure to take the money when he got home. Just to be sure it went to good use. He wanted to visit Mom and let her know he's doing better and I wanted to say my goodbyes.

The day felt a bit cool. A crisp smell hovered nearby, it let me know that autumn neared. A shower had ended moments before, the trees and earth darkened from the drops. I got into my Bug and closed the door. Dad right there with me. I convinced him to let me drive this time. He didn't speak much as we drove down the street and toward the highway with green, lush, and hopeful branches. He cleaned up nicely too. His suit still hung off him a bit. He had showered and slicked his hair back in old school gel. He splashed on Old Spice, the scent which reminded me of Sunday Church and special occasions infused with my vanilla musk air freshener. When he had gotten into the car, I realized he still had on his work boots, freshly mucked from his last job. I guessed some things never changed.

Two blocks from our destination a flower shop called Anne's Treasures had been nestled among other shops. This had been a place that Mama and I had frequented. She would point at the bouquets until she found one that made me smile. She handed the flowers to me so I could smell them. I studied the petals, I touched each one. Mama's soft voice told me to be careful of thorns and thistles, then she picked out her favorites and we returned home, her hand in mine, the other hand held a paper-wrapped bouquet. Dad and I used to go there on Valentine's Day and Mother's Day to pick her up a bouquet. "Do you want to come in?" I asked him.

"You know what she likes." He didn't look at me. His eyes watery, his skin paper thin. Before I got out, he dug into his pockets and handed me a few dollars. "Ya know what? Get her those peach ones. The roses she always loved." I nodded and closed the door.

The shop hadn't changed much since the last time we'd visited. The stone exterior with a blue and white striped overhang, which protected the planted flowers that lined the outside wall. Sunlight radiated through stained glass windows making the floor sparkle with shades of blues, pinks, greens, and yellows. In the corner, among the aisles of flourishing roses, lilacs, baby's breath, I found white petal daisies and Mom's favorite peach roses. I selected our gifts and brought them to the register. The shop owner with gnarled hands wrapped the flowers' stems in blue and green ribbon and then packaged the bouquet in crinkly florist paper.

I handed Dad the flowers and realized he had fallen asleep. No worries. We approached the main entrance of the park. It began with tall stone columns that outlined the gate. An iron archway tinged with rust and dirt crumbled overhead. I decided to let him sleep. He'd know where we were once he woke up. I kept the bouquet of roses with him. Only fair that he give them to her.

I crossed underneath the archway, sure to shield my eyes. The expanse of stones and slabs forced lines in the trimmed grass. Trees knotted and thick with age reached up, their branches intertwined to umbrella and protect the stones below.

A path lit by the morning sun guided me as I walked up to the final place, statues each held a different message for visitors. The signs glistened with drops from the morning storm. I thought others would be visiting their loved ones, but I was the only one there.

I approached the tall cement block that held her. The front covered in a matrix of squares naming the occupants. A dull grey cement bench placed before the mausoleum.

An empty marker next to Mom's for when Dad decided to join her. He had made these arrangements when they were first married. A door-to-door salesman had convinced him that he should make sure my parents were together through eternity. I was surprised to find her marker encrusted in dirt and tinged with rust. Mud had splashed all over the monument from the previous night's rainfall. Patterns of dirt sprayed it. I returned to my car to find my father waking up. "We're here," I said. He opened his eyes and looked around like he was in a totally foreign place. And then the look of acknowledgement. "What're you up to?" he asked. I had slid forward the driver's seat to retrieve Windex and paper towels from the back. "Just going to clean it up a little," I said.

He walked alongside me, bouquet in his hands. I didn't need to comment on the status of the mausoleum, his hand twitched to take the Windex from me.

"You look like a mess," I said. The Windex's crisp scent contrasted against the smell of fresh flowers. My nose twitched. I breathed on the metal to bring up its shine and wiped down the visitor's bench. When I was sure I had returned everything to normal, I took a seat next to Dad. "Looks good," he said. We were quiet for a while. He had a conversation with her, a private one. He nodded here and there and smiled like he relived a favorite moment.

"Lauren's doing great. You'd be proud," he said out loud. "She's still at the diner but sounds like she's going to be a movie star." I hadn't told dad about the work I had done on the movie. I figured he had enough he was trying to do. "We always knew our girl was too big to stay here, didn't we?" He reached over and squeezed my hand.

"Dad? I'm—"

"Mr. P's been glowing about you. Sounds like it's time we let our little girl move on." He got up and kissed Mom's marker. At first I didn't know what to say. I thought that he'd be upset or angry about this. He returned to the seat next to mine. I took a deep breath and then told them about the movie. I told them about Jonathan and about how wonderful he was and how romantic. They knew about him. I had told them about his movies for years, but I needed to let them know he was better in person. They needed to know he was a great man. I told them about the job in California. I was surprised by the excitement in my voice. I hadn't talked to anyone in detail about it but somehow this felt right. A glow of relief came over me as I described my plans.

I needed to know that they listened and they stood with me. I needed my faith to be handed back. In the least, I needed them to tell me everything would be fine. "He sounds like a good man," Dad said. "You're ready for this?"

To be honest, I wasn't sure I was. I mean, I hoped that everything would turn out well but who really knew? What if Lena flaked out and decided not to hire me? What if Jonathan suddenly moved to Tahiti? What if I couldn't find a place to live? I had a hundred what ifs, all of which sounded ridiculous the more I thought of them. "I'll be fine," I said.

In my response I realized I needed reassurance that they wouldn't leave me. Part of me knew this was crazy. Part of me knew that Mama was long gone and that Dad should be fine. He had his crew and even with his friends' faults they still looked after him. Something inside of me needed this. Something inside of me needed to try.

With my last uttered word, I waited. I read and reread Mama's plaque and the ones nearby. I searched the neighboring mausoleums and traced the edges of the angels that guarded each monument. I silently prayed that I would regain my faith. In what, I wasn't sure. I waited for Dad to say something. I got up and put the box before Mom. It contained prayers I had learned as a child. Ones that Mama had taught me. Her favorites. I traced the family tree notes that went back centuries. I closed my eyes to see her. I wanted to feel Mom place her hand on my shoulder.

A breeze wrapped around my legs, twisted up and flew by me. The air tickled my ears and whipped my ponytail. I looked at the plaques. At the tip of my mind, I felt Mama confirm what I needed to know. The fancy lettering twinkled as the sun came from behind a cloud and caressed each name. This happened only for a moment, then the sun disappeared.

"She'd like that," Dad said. "She likes knowing that you're going to be fine."

I rang the doorbell. "Coming!" The door cracked open.

"Lauren. What you doing here?" Mr. P adjusted his glasses. In his hand was a section from the *Sunday Courier Post*.

"I wanted to talk to you and Mrs. P about something." I shoved my hands in my jeans pockets.

"Come in. Come in." He waved me into the house. Seventies style mirrors with specks of gold lame covered the back wall. Mrs. P sat on the black leather couch.

"Lauren. What you doing here?" She got up and kissed me on each cheek. "You want a glass of tea? Fresh made."

"No, thank you. I'm fine." I said.

"You sure? It Mr. P's specialty. He only makes it at home. Don't want customers to get too used to the good stuff." She winked.

"I'm fine. I just came by because I wanted to talk to you about something."

She motioned to the matching loveseat behind me. I sat down and the plastic covering squeaked.

Mr. P took a spot next to the missus. He folded the newspaper on to the top of a stack next to the couch.

"You know how Lena and I have been talking about starting a business?" I began.

"Yes, of course," Mr. P said. "We were there when you read the letter."

"Yes, well. I decided to do it," I said.

Mr. P shifted in his place. Mrs. P sat up straight. Her eyes narrowed as I continued.

"This is the perfect opportunity. How often does someone invite me to start all over in California?"

After a pause Mrs. P yelled, "You're what!"

I nudged away from her. "I'm moving to California," I mumbled.

"Have you lost your mind?" She shot up. Her silhouette reflected in the mirrors next to her. Thousands of Mrs. Ps pointed at me.

"Now Alexandra, this could be good for Lauren." Mr. P took off his glasses and pinched the rim of his nose.

"Don't George. Don't."

She pointed at me. "Do not tell me this has nothing to do with that boy. Do not."

I looked at my lap.

"You moving away for this. Whatever it is. You leave your house, your friends, us. For what?"

"Now, Alexandra let Lauren finish," Mr. P said.

"She finished all right." She paced the length of the room and then went into the kitchen and slammed the refrigerator open and shut. She banged free ice cubes from the freezer and banged kitchen cabinets closed.

"You want this?" He whispered to me.

"Yes," I said.

He got up and went into the kitchen. Their voices elevated. I looked at my reflection dotted with gold specks. The one that grew smaller and smaller the further away it became. Moments later they returned.

"And why are you moving to California, dumping your friends and family here and forgetting about all of us?" She asked.

I considered saying everything. I knew she didn't understand and I didn't want Mr. P to worry.

"I have friends out there. I've got Lena and Zachary and they'll look out for me."

She held a glass of iced tea and sipped from it. "You want me to believe that?" She remained in the hallway between the kitchen and the living room.

"Yes," I said. I looked at Mr. P., only steps behind his wife.

"She'll be fine." He placed his hand on her shoulder. "Don't worry," he said. Mrs. P. walked down the hallway and slammed the door to their bedroom. The photos on the walls bounced and settled off center.

"You need anything, you tell us okay?" Mr. P said.

"Promise."

He straightened the photos and then opened the bedroom door and gently shut it behind him.

We had cleaned up the kitchen, tossed the trash, and left a note for the baker about tomorrow's pastries. Too many glazed and not enough cream filled. I had put away the dishes and silverware while Mrs. P closed out the register. Mrs. P positioned in front of the breaker box in the back of the building. The last item on our list of things to do. I waited for her at the other end of the diner.

"You have everything?" Mrs. P called.

"I think so."

With a click, the back lights went out leaving the orange glow of the emergency exit ablaze. She edged her way toward me. She kept her balance by putting her hand against the wall. I could hear her feet shuffling and then a clunk.

"Damnit."

"What's wrong?" I asked.

Her silhouette scrunched into a ball and then she stood back up.

"Forgot to put the pail away." I heard a thunk against the wall. "I'll take care of it tomorrow."

Alone in the center of the wall, my denim jacket hung next to the front door. I lifted it from its hook. The tag caught and my jacket jerked away. I lifted it again, careful to clear it. I pulled one arm through the sleeve and then the other. I reached for the door when Mrs. P said, "I don't think you should go."

I removed my hand from the word "Push" on the metal plate.

"Why not?" I looked at her.

"Has he responded to your letters?" she asked.

I focused on a square on the floor. "I don't know what you're talking about."

"Don't play with me Lauren, I've known you for years. Has he called you? Visited?" Her voice rose.

"Sorta . . ."

"That means no." She jammed her fist against the table. "Lauren. Don't you see? You're throwing your life away."

"I'm not throwing my life away. He loves me," I whispered.

She glared at me. Her voice darkened. "He doesn't love you, Lauren."

"Yes, he does. How the hell would you know?"

She stepped away from me. "You need to talk civilly."

Only a few more days, I thought. Then I don't have to put up with this anymore. "How can you say that about Jonathan? I know he loves me." I clutched my bag and stepped toward her.

Mrs. P stepped back.

"What's wrong?" I asked.

"You're not yourself. You're not my Lauren."

I moved away from her. "What do you mean?"

Mrs. P edged toward the door. "My Lauren wouldn't leave us." She pushed the door open and walked through the glass door. "My Lauren would be good girl."

"I am still your Lauren." I followed behind her, the glass door cold. "I need to do this."

Mrs. P walked down the steps and to her car. I followed.

"I'll be back," I said.

Mrs. P unlocked the door and got in. She placed her purse in the passenger seat and closed the door.

"I promise. I'll be back."

She turned the key in the ignition. The Pontiac choked and then the engine chugged on.

"No. My Lauren will never be back." She drove away.

Door ajar behind me. I had packed my clothes and put my most important items in my new keepsake box. Dad had met me for breakfast. His cheeks flushed, for once he looked happy. He had gotten a call for another job at the docks. His buddy said he'd pick up Dad at 9 a.m. sharp. He woke me up with a huge breakfast of eggs, pork roll, English muffins and orange juice. I didn't even know we had all of that in the house. He gobbled every bite on his plate and every once in a while looked at me with a pride I don't remember seeing before. He kissed me on the cheek and said that he loved me. "I love you too, Dad." I hugged him and kept myself from crying. I never thought I'd cry. I closed the front door with a soft slam. Sure not to turn my head, I held my luggage at my sides, my box nuzzled safely under my arm.

Autumn had arrived. The crisp scent of fallen leaves and turned earth replaced the humidity of summer. I had called Mr. P to see if he could give me a ride. Rich must have been in the restaurant because the next thing I knew he had been volunteered to take me to the airport.

Across the street, Rich waited in his black Corvette. I had given my VW to my dad. I figured he could keep it or sell it or do whatever he needed to do with it. "Ready?" Rich asked. He leaned against the car in that suave way that only former jocks and popular kids know how to do. As he came towards me, I noticed a slight awkwardness or uncertainty that I had never seen before. He took my bags and loaded them into the trunk. He didn't look at me. He hadn't looked at me the same since the day he asked me to the movies. I still felt guilty about that. I got in the passenger's side. We pulled away. I refused to look at the house. Afraid that I'd see ghosts of myself as a child. In the corner of my eye my mother waved goodbye. I gazed at the road before us, fascinated by the traffic lights.

Along the highway's rim, the trees started to change. The burnt oranges, warm yellows, and aged browns fell with a whisper and left the tree behind to fend through the upcoming winter. Crisp dryness accompanied the fall. A hint of cold kissed my cheeks as it came in through the cracked window.

The area that lined the highway changed from trees to cement the closer we got to the airport. Tall barriers blocked my view of the towns. We followed a curving road to signs that pointed in every direction. Luckily, Rich knew the way.

He stopped the car in front of the California Airlines baggage check-in sign. It loomed overhead and swayed in the breeze. A tinny voice came through a round speaker that looked like a bull-horn. The words barely audible.

I had never flown before. Rich handed me a pack of gum when I got out of the car. "Chew this while you're taking off. It'll help with the poppin'," he said.

Cars raced in and out. A compact Ford illegally parked, a quick embrace, a sorrowful goodbye and then the driver disappeared back into the car and whisked away down the curving road. I was simply one among many lugging bags filled with personal possessions and promised presents. A porter approached the future passenger and offered to assist.

A high screech came from the direction of the runway. Another plane took off. Rich took my bags out of the trunk.

"This is what you want?" he asked.

I wanted to say, *of course this is what I want. Who wouldn't want this?* Instead I said, "This is what I want." I held my hand out. "Thanks for driving me. I know Mr. P appreciated it."

He held his arms out. My arms intertwined with his. I could feel the muscles in his back. We had never been this close before. I felt his heart beating, felt his warmth. For a moment, I became lost in it. His hands rubbed my back and I reciprocated. I nudged my face into the crook of his neck, my lips brushed his skin. He smelled of Ivory soap, hair gel, and musky deodorant. Then I remembered why I was there and let go.

"Thanks for the ride," I said to his feet.

"No problem," he responded. I headed for the full-length rotating glass doors. "Look. About the other day," he said.

"I'm sorry," I said before he continued. I looked up at him.

"I wanted to tell you it would have been cool to go to the movies."

"Oh." I shifted the cardboard box under my arm.

"What I mean is. It's cool, you know. You do what you got to do." He dug his hands into his pockets. He shrugged and got back into his car.

I didn't think I'd miss Rich. Even though we were never close, he was always there, in some way. I waved as he drove off. He arched his neck as he peered into the rearview mirror.

The rotating doors opened into a vast entry. Along the back wall, customer service agents assisted travelers. Passengers snaked in a maze to check in. People bustled and dragged bags of belongings and gifts. Children with desperate eyes hurried behind their parents. I wandered in with the hope of finding my flight. I stopped before a panel of screens detailing the flights and their arrival and departure times. The times flickered and changed to "arrived" or "on time" or "delayed." I found my flight number and began my trek down the terminal. A map showed that the airport was in the shape of an E and I stood at the bottom end of the vertical line. I needed to get to the end of the middle horizontal line. I made my way through the crowds and checked the map to confirm that I headed in the right direction.

The hall lined with shops—a sunglass cart; a candy stand with M&M's, Philly pretzels, chocolate chip cookies, mints, and gum; a stand with CD players for rent and CDs for sale. A family of four rested on a bench. The oldest daughter held a crying baby while her brother wore headphones and bopped to music. Their parents dug through bags in search of something. A man dressed in a grey suit carried a day bag and a woman in a black suit clutched a leather briefcase and rushed through the terminal. "Excuse me," she called from behind. I stepped out of the way, afraid she would run me over.

I found my gate. At the customer service desk, the agent, Mai-Len, offered to assist. Around her neck she wore a blue, green, and brown striped scarf, which matched her brown uniform and green eyes. She took my ticket and driver's license and typed on her keyboard.

"It looks to be on time," she said. She tapped more keys and then looked up. "Sorry. Looks like it's been delayed in Chicago. An unexpected storm. We'll start calling for passengers to board as soon as the plane is here."

"Is there another flight?" I asked. Lena would be waiting for me at the other end. She had agreed to pick me up at the airport and warned me that we had errands to do. I just wanted to get through the flight.

She typed again and picked up a black phone. "California Air," she answered. After a few minutes she said, "The next flight isn't until later this evening."

"Never mind," I said and thanked her.

In the area before the gate were rows of blue plastic seats bolted to the ground. I picked up my carry-on package and found a place to rest. I held my keepsake box to my chest.

Mai-Len called over the speaker for a Mrs. Jones and a Mr. Harrod. She reminded us of the flight delay and asked for volunteers to be bumped to a later flight. A gentleman next to me got up and approached the counter.

Mrs. P was still mad when I left. After we closed the diner she hadn't spoken to me again. I had called. Mr. P answered. "The missus is out right now," he had said.

"Tell her I'll miss her." We said our goodbyes. As always, he said, "You know you'll have a place here, if you want."

I unpeeled the silver paper from a powdery stick of chewing gum. Its sweet mint flavor coated my mouth. Lena and I had talked about her new catering business but I didn't know what to expect.

"I'm finally breaking out on my own," she had said. "I can't do this by myself. And you need to get the heck out of Jersey." She had laughed. I laughed too even though I knew it was true.

"Welcome to California Air. We will begin boarding flight 341 in five minutes," the agent said over the speaker. People jammed in front of each other. The stewardess called row numbers to begin boarding the flight. I followed the rest of the passengers in line. The stewardess took my ticket and abruptly ripped it in two and glanced at my photo ID to confirm that, yes, I was the Lauren Scott scheduled to board this plane. She recited my seat number and told me to have a nice day. I almost choked on the scent of her flowery perfume.

I entered the cone-shaped hall that stunk like the inside of a shoe. It ended at a cave-like entry. At the door, a woman greeted me and reaffirmed my seat number. The width of the aisle barely fit one person. Passengers jammed in front of me. We waited while a guy my age loaded his bags in an upper compartment. I followed the tight aisle and breathed deeply to force the walls back.

I found my seat in the back, a window seat. This was my first time flying and I wanted to see the world from above.

A woman sat in the middle seat. She gripped the armrests, her hands turned stark white. "Excuse me," I said. Without getting up, she shifted her body, moved her legs in closer. I squeezed by, the knob of the table tray jabbed my back.

I strapped into the seat, obeyed the instructions given by the stewardess over the intercom. She demonstrated how to put on a life vest and use the flotation cushion, where to find the nearest exit, and how to use the oxygen mask. I reread the instructions, in case I missed a detail. Other planes took off and began their journeys. I wondered what passengers did inside those aircrafts. Where they went. Did they follow a dream or start a new life? Or only continue with one they had? I wondered how many knew what their futures held and what would happen to them in the next day, month, or year. I slid my box underneath the seat before me, sure that it was within view.

I heard the scream of engines from outside. Their pitch heightened as the plane began its trek along the runway. The plane vibrated with the movement. A soft hum of air swirled from overhead. Re-filtered air came out of the vents. A beep sounded. The fasten seat belts sign glowed red. I verified that my seat belt was secured. The plane's pace quickened and then weightlessness and the pull of gravity hit me. My stomach and feet lifted from their spots while my back and head pinned to my chair. I turned to see the airport become smaller and smaller below me. Clouds blurred my view. I unwrapped another stick of gum and folded it into my mouth. I chewed feverishly, sure not to being experiencing whatever popping Rich talked about. I was amazed at how the world looked from above. No wonder everyone wanted to go to heaven.

The woman next to me pinched her face, her lips shut, her eyes glued closed. Her body a pole against the seat. She became a statue desperate for the ride to end.

"Ma'am?" I reached out to tap her on the shoulder but hesitated. "Ma'am. It's not so bad. See?" I said these words softly so she heard them but not so loudly that she became more frightened. "Ma'am?" I whispered. She shook her head like she tried to get rid of a bug that wouldn't leave her alone. One that buzzed around her ears.

“The view is amazing,” I said. I hoped she heard. I hoped that maybe she would become curious and open one eye. Just one. I thought the sight of the world outside might lift her spirits like it did mine.

“Are you going to be all right?” I asked. She whipped her head back and forth like she had a convulsion. Stewardesses swayed with the plane’s movement as they pushed a clattering drink cart down the aisle.

“May I take your order?” asked the stewardess, dressed in a uniform similar to the one I wore for the movie. Before I could ask for a soda, the woman next to me reached into her shirt pocket and shoved money at her. The bills crinkled like waste paper.

“Triple vodka.” She ordered. She barely moved her lips. The stewardess served us our drinks and gave us small packets of honey roasted peanuts and lightly salted pretzels. I scarfed down the snacks. Traveling must have made me hungry. The woman shot back the vodka and returned to her almost stationary position.

“Are you okay?” I asked once she had finished her drink.

Her hands shook. “Leave me alone.”

“I just.”

“Leave me the hell alone.”

She shot a blood-lined look at me. Suddenly I felt nauseas. I didn’t know if it was from the flight or the motion or having this crazy lady sitting next to me. I fumbled with the seatbelt, grabbed my box, and climbed over her.

“Keep your big mouth *shut*.” She growled.

I raced to the bathroom, latched it closed and flung up the toilet lid. What was I doing? Was I insane? What if Lena wasn’t there? Or Jonathan? What if he hated me? The contents of my stomach rushed forward. I crumbled onto the floor and fumbled to open the box. The lid fought me. I pried my fingers between the lid and its base when it opened a crack and then with a ssshhhhh the lid tore at the edge and flipped open. I gripped the comb. I felt its teeth against my fingertips and clutched it to my chest. My breathing slowed. I rested on the bathroom floor and placed my head against my arm.

At baggage claim, Lena held a sign made from tan cardboard, the word "Welcome" scribbled in felt tipped black marker. She outlined the letters in yellow, the black smudged and created grey pools. When she saw me, she dropped the sign. "Heeyyy!" She flung open her arms. Her jeans ripped in strategic places. Her Runaways t-shirt hung off of one shoulder and revealed the strap of a neon blue bra. I dropped my bags as she pulled me into a hug. I lost my breath in her arms. "How was the flight?" she asked.

"It was fine," I coughed. Still tired from the six hour flight, I wasn't sure of the proper thing to say.

"Turbulent?" she asked.

"It was fine." I forced a smile. She picked up one of my bags and pointed to an exit.

She punched my arm. "This's gonna rock."

We walked through what felt like a long winding tunnel. The main difference from the airport in Philadelphia was that this one had advertisements for Las Vegas and Santa Fe compared to Philly's ads for Atlantic City.

As the automatic doors slid open, Lena put on her sunglasses. A burst of dry hot air greeted us. She laughed. "You'll get used to that. We'll pick you up a pair of shades at the store. You'll need them."

I stripped off my wool cardigan. The heat of California broke through the cloth, my shirt and bra stuck to my body. Rows and rows of cars stacked in diagonal lines before us. She walked right into the closest entrance and weaved her way through the mass of cars. She stopped at a white truck, similar to the one she had in

Jersey. The words, *Metal Rocks!* hung from the rearview mirror. The California license plate seemed to be the newest item on the worn vehicle. I rested on the frame. I only wanted to sleep.

"You won't need that for a while." Lena tossed my sweater and bags into the back. "Hope you don't mind. We've got some errands to run before we stop home."

"Really?" I moaned.

"Don't worry, this won't take long."

With the words *this won't take long* I tried to perk up.

"If you're really tired, you can wait in the car. I won't be long."

"That's okay. I want to help." I smiled and then straightened up. We hopped into the truck. The passenger side seat had been ripped and repaired with duct tape. I sat on what must have been a loose spring. "Buckle up," she said as she fastened the safety strap across her chest and clicked it into place.

We exited the parking garage. The freeway stretched and curled and spread for what looked like an eternity. Cars sped past us and then jolted to a stop. Mopeds slinked through, winding their way between cars. I don't know why but the highway felt longer and more turbulent than the highways in New Jersey. As if we had been catapulted into a stunt driving show. No one seemed to pay attention to each other, which on a ten-lane highway is a little bit of a problem. Lena blew her horn in frustration. "Who does that guy think he is?" she yelled at a motorcycle that had weaved between our truck and the car in front of us. I shrugged, not sure what to say. The heat caused waves to form on the concrete. A truck that looked like it had been constructed of leftover parts from vehicles starting in the 1960s chugged before us. Piled with lawn equipment, I hoped the shifting materials didn't flop out of their truck and onto ours. Lena slid out from behind him and up a few lanes as soon as she had the chance.

Once we broke through the deadlock, she tossed the truck across the highway and tore through an exit. I gripped the pleather armrest and closed my eyes, afraid that the truck would overturn.

"You should see me when there aren't any cars on the road."

Off the exit amassed an oversized building with a huge Price Club sign in front. The place reminded me of Costco, one of the bulk purchasing clubs. Tons of people came and went with oversized and overloaded shopping carts. We parked a football field length away from the main entrance. Lena hopped out of the car. "Come on." I dragged myself out. Each one of my steps felt leaden. She speed-walked to the door and grabbed an orange plastic cart, one for each of us. I listened on as she chattered about her latest gigs and the cheapest happy hours and the nicest clubs. My mind jumbled it all together under the haze of airsickness and lack of sleep.

"Here," she wheeled one my way and disappeared through the automatic doors. I tagged behind her, focusing on her feet to guide me in the right direction. I had goosebumps within seconds of entering the store. The aisles were wide like the freeways. I followed Lena into the first aisle. She eyeballed the prepackaged pastry snacks. Even though I had shopped with the Ps and of course they had a supplier for their fresh products, I had never seen anything quite like this before. Rows of televisions and radios. Aisles dedicated to condiments. Another aisle focused on breakfast cereal. I never knew so many products existed.

"Everyone has special requests. This time Justine wants Twinkies on demand. Who would think those buggers were popular?" Mr. P refused to carry Twinkies or any kind of pastry that was prepackaged in the Oaklyn. He insisted that everything on hand at the diner was either made on-site or by a local business.

We loaded the bottom of the food cart with boxes of golden snack cakes. "Justine eats Twinkies whenever she's nervous. Rumor has it that the studio will put her on a diet every other week because she'll balloon up like that." She snapped her fingers. I nodded, sure to stay behind her so she had access to my cart. "Normally, I have the produce and meat suppliers take care of everything but for stuff like this, sometimes it's easier to pick it up in bulk at Price Club," she said.

We made our way through the aisles. Lena selected what we needed and what she thought we might need for the upcoming week. I lagged behind, amazed at the different products. I had never seen an aisle dedicated to ethnic or vegetarian foods. In aisle number twelve I stopped moving.

"What's your deal?" She called from across the way. I knew for people from California that this wasn't a big deal. Coming from the East Coast where Prohibition wasn't just taken seriously but the remnants of Prohibition era laws still existed, to seeing the glittering bottles and brightly colored boxes of wine, beer, and hard liquor in a grocery store was unheard of. And yet, here they were in the aisle next to snack foods.

"We can't get this in Jersey. At least not in the grocery store."

Lena laughed. "You're not in Kansas anymore Toto."

She grabbed my arm and guided me toward the dairy aisle. She checked off item after item on her list while sharing her plans for us in the next few weeks—both workwise and fun. "Let's go sightseeing. I never did that. Just because I live here don't mean I've seen everything."

"Really?" When I thought about it, I never ran up the steps of the Museum of Art famous in the *Rocky* movies but every tourist visiting Philadelphia has. Never saw the Liberty Bell either, well, except for when I was in the first grade.

We waited in line with our carts loaded to twice their intended size. When the clerk rang us up I could have passed out.

"No problem," Lena said as she wrote a check out to the store. "This ain't nothing. Just wait till you see the distributor's bill, then you can look bug-eyed."

We loaded the groceries into the back of the truck. "Next stop, home." She announced.

I didn't have much to say on the ride home. At this point I really just wanted to crawl into bed. I tried to register everything but I guess I was still in a daze from the flight.

She parked the truck in front of three apartment buildings clustered together. The center building was made of stucco and curved in a U shape with a courtyard in the center. A dried up, hard water stained fountain was the centerpiece. Spouts surrounded by shells marked where the water once flowed. The building to the left had folding chairs set up underneath windows, which gave the feeling of being at a shore house. The building to the right had hanging plants with bright red and golden flowers that blossomed and curled down leafy vines.

The main floor apartments had little gardens of flowers and herbs. Doors had welcome signs hanging underneath the small magnifying peepholes that allowed owners to see out but wouldn't let visitors see in.

Lena grabbed a few boxes and lugged them to a first floor apartment that had drawn curtains. I followed suit. A black welcome mat with the word, "Yo" in white lay in front of the door. She pulled out a long chain of keys that jingled. The key to her front door chimed among the dozens of others. I glimpsed the inside of her place before going in. She drew the curtains open and let the limited light from the courtyard into the main room.

"It's nothing special," she said. "But it's home." The light shone into a living room that had an adjoining dinette and a half kitchen. A small hallway ended with her bedroom. "You'll sleep here." She nudged toward the couch and put down her bags. She yanked on a thick cord until a foldaway bed came up from under the sofa's cushions. She strained harder until the supporting legs clunked onto the floor. "At least you can stay here till you get a place of your own." It didn't look too bad. We sat on the bed. It felt a little lumpy but she let me stay for free so I guessed I couldn't complain. Besides, the wooing sensation of nearly being in a horizontal position almost had me pass out.

"Great. Thank you," I said.

"The landlord said an efficiency was opening up across the way in a month or so. We can head over to the office tomorrow and talk to him if you want." Lena got up and started to put away the groceries. A storage freezer and an extra fridge monopolized the living room, barely leaving space for the sofa.

"What's all that for?" I asked.

"I know, it's crazy. Just for extra supplies until I can find a decent place to base my business. This will have to do for now."

"We're going to do everything here?" I asked and got up, suddenly understanding that we had an entire truck to unload.

"Well, kind of. I rented a space that has an industrial kitchen a little ways from here but we can't keep the supplies there. I'll get my own space soon. You know, once things are settled. I have my eye on a few places. No worries."

No worries. For some reason those words made me worry. I thought when she said she had started her own business that meant she had an office with an industrial sized kitchen. I guessed I had a lot to learn. I picked up her truck keys and retrieved the last of the groceries. I wanted to get this done as soon as possible. When we finished, we had overfilled the storage spaces. Thankfully we had found a spot for all of the perishables.

"Are you sure about this?" I sat on a stool in the kitchen. "I mean, isn't this kind of weird?" I had a teensy realization that I sounded an awful lot like Mrs. P. Just enough to make me want to take those words back.

"Nah. Lots of catering businesses started this way. Look at *Porto's* down the road. They started out of the owner's kitchen. Same with *Sweet Lady Jane*. We'll be fine. We're in with some greats."

"Okay."

"I forgot to tell you," she said. "A box came for you yesterday." I had packed everything I didn't think I'd use like Mama's figurines and Dad's old tie clip and then mailed it all to Lena. I socked away everything I had brought with me. Lena's continued activity in the kitchen let me know that we had a lot more work ahead of us. I dragged my butt next to her. In her hand was a list of sandwiches, salads, and other goodies we needed to prepare. "This is for tomorrow. If you want, grab a quick nap and then you can help out."

Although the thought of resting was incredibly enticing, I decided against it. After everything Lena had done for me, the least I could do was wait a little bit before conking out. "What should we do first?" She rinsed a fresh head of leafy crisp lettuce in the sink. "You can start with these." She tossed a bunch of carrots and celery at me. "We need those in stick form." Then she turned on the radio to a local rock station. Scorpion's *Rock You Like a Hurricane* blasted through the speakers. "Just you and me kid."

We rinsed and chopped cucumbers, tomatoes, pineapple, papaya, avocado. Pretty much everything we could get our hands on. We mixed salads and prepped the sandwiches and salads. Once she felt comfortable enough with our work, meaning she figured we could pretty much grab and go whatever we needed for tomorrow, we watched television on the sixteen-inch black and white screen. She had placed it on a small card table that subbed as a dining room and a kitchen table. I begged out and laid down on the fold out.

I heard her click through the channels. Sounds of news and *Wheel of Fortune* and then she turned on *Entertainment This*

Moment, evident from their theme song. Jane Marogo dished on the latest news about George Michael and Madonna. My eyelids closed, no matter how hard I resisted. Jane gushed over Julia Roberts's dress at the Golden Globes and pooh-poohed the way Eric Stoltz avoided the media at his latest premiere. "You should see this," Lena said. "It's really killer." I whispered something that I thought was, "That sounds great" but I think it came out more like some inaudible nonsense. After the commercial break, Jane started again. "That's right, the long awaited movie, *Jersey Diner* will premiere later this week, and we'll have the scoop first." My eyes shot open to see Jane Marogo pose in front of a poster with a small diner reminiscent of a train car in the center of a green field and head shots of Jonathan and Dianne anchoring the top corners.

"You got here just in time," Lena said.

"What do you mean?" Were we invited to the premiere? I needed to buy a new outfit. I had heard that if you were in a film then you were invited to stuff like that but I kind of ignored it because it seemed too good to be true.

"I'm just messin' with you." I guess it was. I slinked back into the couch.

"What's wrong? Oh. No. They don't invite the *little people* to those things. And we are definitely little." Lena snickered.

I curled into a ball. "Not to walk on the red carpet or anything . . ."

"I'll tell you what." I heard Lena open and close the refrigerator. She must have been finishing up. "When it comes out, we'll go see it. You can see yourself on the big screen."

Chapter 18

I dressed in Lena's bedroom, which consisted of two windows that reminded me of something from a drive-thru, wall closets with mirrors for doors, a full bed on the floor and a dresser directly across from the bed. The brown carpeting had matted chunks that formed a path to the bed, dresser and closets. Posters from bands like The Cure, Metallica, the Ramones, and Mötley Crüe hung on the alabaster walls. Bands postured and posed in black with hair dyed to match.

I carefully laid out my clothes. I chose black so I looked slim and sophisticated. Even if I didn't walk the red carpet, I knew Jonathan would see me in the crowd. After Mrs. P's reaction I learned to mention Jonathan as little as possible. I made sure to keep conversations with Lena focused on her business and topics of interest to her.

I brushed on pink nail polish and used lots of lotion on my chapped hands. I checked myself in the mirror and turned to make sure nothing stuck out like toilet paper or a sales tag. Although Jonathan said he liked my innocence, I didn't think this attraction extended to being unkempt.

"Where you going, Hot Stuff?" Lena entered the room. She chewed on a slice of pizza. For someone who cooked really well, she sure did order a lot of pizza. She said that when she got off of work, she didn't want to cook.

"Just thought I'd check out what's around. Can I borrow this?" A silver chain with a crystal phoenix hung over the dresser. I held it to the light and refractions of color sung from the detailed edges. The phoenix's head faced upward. Its wings spread, as if in flight. Its claws escaped a fire of gold that burst from below.

"I don't know. That's one of my faves." She admired the necklace and then looked at me. "If you really want it, then okay. But you need to bring it back. It's one of a kind." She flopped onto the bed, wiped crust crumbs from the red and black striped bedspread.

"Isn't tonight the premiere?" Lena picked up a newspaper splayed across the comforter.

"I don't know. Is it?" I played with the necklace's clasp, avoided her gaze. As I placed the necklace around my neck, I realized its size. The phoenix sat perfectly in the center of my chest, the necklace a centerpiece.

"Yeah. According to this newspaper." She flipped the page and glanced at me.

"I didn't notice." I sprayed a cloud of cologne in the air and walked through it.

"Huh." She flipped a page. "If you're going to the premiere, you don't have to lie about it."

"I'm not lying. I'm going sightseeing, that's all."

"I thought we were going sightseeing this weekend." Lena chomped on the last of her pizza. I grew woozy from the smell. I hadn't eaten all day. I wanted to be slim for tonight.

"We are. I'm just checkin' out a few things on my own, that's all. We'll do lots of sightseeing this weekend."

"Look, Lauren." Lena eased off the bed. "I know you really want to see Jonathan and all . . ."

"I don't want to see Jonathan."

"In a slinky black dress, pumps, and . . ."

"Look, can we drop this? I thought I'd look nice when I went out. What's wrong with that?" I couldn't believe she made such a big deal out of it. Why did she care where I went? "We work like crazy. Sometimes I just want to look nice."

"'Kay. If that's how you want to play it. Fine." She marched out of her bedroom. Her demeanor told me that I was officially the employee and she was *the* Boss. "I'll see you tomorrow morning. Bright and early. We have a shoot in the afternoon. Last minute gig."

"No problem."

"I can't have you falling asleep . . ."

"Don't worry about me. I'll be fine." The tail ends of her pant legs flapped visibly as she left the room. Who did she think she was? I knew exactly what I was doing. I felt my purse, the bottle bulged from inside, the comb tucked in a side pocket. I felt for the comb's teeth and grazed my thumb against it then pressed the pad of my thumb into the indentations of his initials.

Zach stopped by and offered to take us out. "Welcome you to LA," he said as he gave me a hug. An intimate hug like the one Rich had given me the last time I saw him. Zach's actions confused me. I swore he was gay when we first met but the longer I knew him, the more I questioned my assumptions.

"She has plans." Lena rolled her eyes. "I'm free. Let's jet." She tossed her bag over her shoulder and headed for the front door.

For a second Zach looked disappointed but then he shrugged. "You look fantastic. Another time?"

Two minutes after they left I headed to the bus stop to get to Mann's Chinese Theatre. I felt a little awkward dressed up while getting on the bus. I felt even more awkward when a bum sat next to me. Great. Hopefully his smell wouldn't somehow transfer onto my clothes. He leaned closer to me and reached forward as if he wanted to touch my necklace. I swear he mumbled "pretty" so I immediately got up and sat behind the bus driver. The bum stayed in place and looked disappointed. I quickly looked away, hoping that if I acted like he didn't exist then maybe he'd leave me alone. Luckily, I only had two more stops to my destination. Just as the bum got up the driver called out my street and I hopped off as fast as possible.

The sheer darkness of the evening surprised me. I'd watched TV specials thousands of times and I swore premieres happened during the day. I stopped at a corner market to buy a bottle of water. I turned the corner to find a huge crowd of people that jammed the area for blocks. I nudged my way closer to the crowd's center. Stadium style stands held fans above the red carpet. I eased my way forward, one step at a time.

"Where do you think you're going?" A man in denim asked.

"I'm late?" I bit my lower lip.

"Right. Late. I think you better . . ."

"Gotta go." I shoved my way farther into the crowd. The closer I got to the theater, the denser the crowd became. Even with the blocked view, a patch of light came through. Searchlights rotated, bringing attention to the exact spot I needed.

"Ow! What the hell are you doing?" Yelled a woman with streaked blonde hair. She wore a tight pink dress with four inch red heels. She pulled my arm. Her face, plastered in makeup, contorted. She took off her shoe. Its heel had torn away from the base. She waved the shoe in my face.

"You did this," she said.

"Sorry. I'm sorry." I tried to get away but she yanked on my sleeve so hard that it tore.

"I don't think so."

I apologized again and offered her money to have the shoe repaired. She refused and wouldn't let me go. I hoped to convince her that I had a great reason for getting in front of her.

"You don't understand. I'm IN the movie. I know Jonathan and Dianne. We are really, really close, so if you just . . ."

"Right. And I'm Brooke Shields's sister. Don't. Fuck. With. Me." She lightly punched me in the arm with each word.

I winced. "I'm not. You want to find out, then you can come up there with me and I can prove it to you."

"Yeah right."

A man next to us shoved his way through. He almost knocked her over. "Hey!" She reached for him. I took the chance to pull away from her and into another direction.

"Where the f—? Don't worry. I'll find you." She threatened then took off her other shoe and ran after the man.

I maneuvered my way through the rest of the crowd, careful where I walked. Once I broke free from the masses, the lights flooded before me. The red carpet was brighter than I had imagined. Searchlights shone on the immediate area, the carpet awash in glow. I placed my hands over my eyes.

Next to me a security guard blocked the way. He wore a black jacket with green lettering, "Jersey Diner" in script across the back. A curlycue of wire curved around his ear. His muscular arms fought against the jacket's fabric. His thick neck reminded me of a tree trunk. Something about the way he stood told me that no one wanted to be near him and for good reasons. Sure not to touch him, I searched the crowd for someone familiar. Lena wasn't kidding when she said they didn't invite the crew to the event.

"Excuse me." I introduced myself to the guard and explained my situation. He didn't look at me. He looked like he was about to laugh. I don't know why he wanted to laugh.

Someone from behind pushed me and I fell into the guard. "Sorry," she called over her shoulder. Those fans were crazy. They crushed into each other to get near a famous person. That didn't do anything. They didn't know Jonathan.

"I'm sorry," I said to the guard. He glanced at me for a split second. "I just. I mean. I know I'm not supposed to be here so." What was the point? He wasn't going to let me stay. "You know what? Never mind. It's okay."

"Look. You can stand here but don't do anything," he said. "This area is for Press. Just don't be obvious."

"Thanks," I said. I wanted to ask him *why are you doing this? Why be so nice to me?* But then I figured it was probably best not to push my luck. And then he answered my silent question. "It'd be easier to keep you here rather than try to get you over there." He pointed to the stadium seating. With the size and density of the crowd I had no idea how I would have gotten there. "Where you're supposed to be."

"I'm sorry. I didn't know . . ."

Lights flashed and bulbs popped. Photographers and reporters called, "Jonathan! Over here! Jonathan!" I was shoved into the guard again.

Jonathan needed to see me. If he saw me for a second, I knew he would call me over. Jonathan's back to me, he waved at the mountains of fans that cried for his attention.

People tossed autograph books and pens at him. He scribbled his name and smiled. He shook hands. Waved. Posed for pictures. He was alone except for his assistant. She remained a dozen feet behind him.

He must have gotten my letter saying I would be there. Finally, I thought. If only he saw me. I called out, "Jonathan, it's me. Lauren! Jonathan!" He turned. I waved, "Jonathan!" So many others tried to gain his attention. Our eyes almost met and I lost my footing. I continued to wave and leaned forward over the roped area.

"Jonathan! It's Lauren! I'm here!" The guard put his arm out and lightly moved me back behind the roping. Jonathan's eyes narrowed. He had to have seen me. He waved to the crowd again. His assistant adjusted her glasses and then touched him on his arm and whispered something. He nodded. His attention gone. "No, no. Jonathan! It's me. Me!"

"Jonathan! Jonathan!" The crowd parroted.

Camera lights flashed and exploded. His shadow floated down the red carpet and dissolved behind thick black doors.

"I need to talk to him," I told the security guard. "I'm serious. I know him."

He frowned. I tried to find another way, any way, to get inside that theater. A jade-like statue of a Chinese dragon hovered over the entry. I grabbed hold of the dragon's arm and lifted up.

"I don't think so young lady." A hand pulled at the bottom of my dress. I looked down to see the same guard yanking on the fabric.

"You don't understand. Jonathan." I screamed. Jonathan came out of the theater for a moment and looked around. Finally.

"Up here." I cried. His assistant came out and said something to him. I clutched the necklace and hoped it hadn't disappeared. Jonathan faded back inside. I couldn't believe it. "Wait! It's me. It's me." My arms grew weak as did my spirit. He couldn't hear me. I pushed off the statue and nearly fell on top of the guard.

In one hand, I gripped the phoenix and in the other I clung to my purse. People pushed and shoved until I became engulfed in the crowd. One among millions.

Chapter 19

Tents and trailers parked in a circle. Sheets of fabric blew in the desert breeze with clusters of workers huddled underneath the cloth's shadow. Workers dotted the sand. Beyond us, dunes formed and framed the valley. Another traveling city, but not as nice as *Jersey Diner*'s set up.

Small white plastic fans whirred inside the catering truck. The dry heat pulled perspiration from my skin. My ponytail ends floated in the breeze. Lena's hair plastered in gel, looked one color instead of its signature two-tone. She took a cool damp cloth and pressed it against the back of her neck.

"Hand me the ketchup?" Lena held her hand out. I picked up the bottle shaped like a tomato and put it in her palm. "Harold. Your order's up," she said. Harold, one of the grips, had been working with us for a while. Even on the first day he had been one of the chattiest crewmembers. Harold had been trying to get Lena to talk to him for the last half-hour. He noticed that Lena refused to speak to me. Instead she talked to everyone around me and asked them to speak to me on her behalf. "I can't believe she won't speak to you," he had said. "You're inseparable." I hadn't thought about it until he had said it but I guess Harold was right. We had been inseparable, at least until the other night.

"Thanks, Lena. Don't you think . . ."

"I know what I'm doing, Harold."

"She looks like she needs someone to talk to." Harold motioned to me. His favorite haunt was the catering truck, evident by his paunch.

"She doesn't need anyone but Jonathan." Lena rolled her eyes.

"That's not fair." Harold said and took a bite from his egg and cheese on a long roll.

"It's okay, Harold." I wiped down the grill, removing bits of egg.

"Stay out of it, Harold." Lena packed her cigarettes onto the counter.

"Harold, you don't have to defend me," I said.

"What would you say if you were—" he said to Lena.

"Stay out—" Lena warned.

"I'm just saying that—"

"I'm telling you, grab your sandwich and get away." She pointed at his camera.

Harold looked like she had punched him in the face. "You got it," he said and returned to his place next to camera four.

Harold wanted everyone to be the best of friends. We had nicknamed him The Peacekeeper even though this time Lena didn't listen to him.

"Excuse me." Lena nudged by me. The hollow door to the trailer crashed closed as the room shook. The moment her foot hit the sand she lit a cigarette. The smell of freshly lit tobacco seeped through the door. I made wide circles with the cloth, sure to wipe down every inch of counter space. I concentrated on the circular movement. I felt for the smoothness of clean.

When I got home the night before, Lena had been asleep. The apartment dark and still, I dropped onto the couch and covered my head with pillows and burrowed into the cushions. I thought if I could disappear inside the cushions then the pain would go away. I held the pillow against my head, letting the feathers jab my face. I hoped they would puncture my skin and let me feel something other than this pain; the pain of being invisible. I pressed the pillow deeper and deeper against me. It became hot with my exhales.

I couldn't get the image of Jonathan out of my head. I had cried and yelled out to him, desperate for him to take one look at me. My throat became raw with it. His head never turned, he never blinked in my direction.

"Come on. Get up." Lena had tapped my arm. It throbbed with pain. I pulled up the sleeve to find blues, browns, and purples.

"Jesus, Lauren. What the hell were you doing last night?" She loomed over me in black cotton short-shorts and a cotton t-shirt that said, *Star Wars Rules*.

I thought about telling her. I really did. The entire time I walked home I had rehearsed what to say. "I know I said I wouldn't go but I had to see Jonathan. I swear, if he had seen me then he would have . . ." I never thought out the entire conversation because the more I practiced it, the longer it got and the more complicated it became. Silence was best.

"You won't even tell me that? Jesus, Lauren. You look like someone beat you." Lena went into the kitchen and cracked ice from a tray, then put it into a plastic bag and handed it to me. "Put this on, it might help numb the bruise."

"Thanks." I held the package against my arm. The coldness shocked my skin and reduced the pain. My head throbbed.

"You just wouldn't listen, would you?" she asked.

"I don't know . . ."

"Don't." An unlit cigarette dangled between her two fingers. "You don't think I know how to turn on a TV?" She pointed at the black and white. "I saw you. I. Saw. You." She leaned into the sink. "Your butt hung off a statue."

"TV?" The word cleared my head. I looked down at the bruises. I couldn't look at her.

"I'm going to shower. Be ready for work." She crushed the cigarette into an ashtray and left the room. "I want my necklace back."

I held the phoenix that rested against my chest and then kissed the clasp for good luck and took it off.

She didn't talk to me the entire ride to the shoot. I bet half the crew saw it. I prepared the morning spread when Carol, a production assistant, came up to me. "That was so friggin' funny. Like, what made you think to do that?"

"What?" I laid out blueberry muffins, glazed donuts, and bagels.

"I mean it was obviously a joke right? I mean, like, wow the cameras just loved you." She took one of the blueberry muffins and nibbled its edge.

"Yeah. A joke." Lena came out of the truck, carrying a tray of freshly cut strawberries, melon, and cantaloupe.

"Was it like performance art or something?" Carol asked.

Lena thumped the tray next to the pastries.

"I thought it'd be funny," I told her. Lena went back into the trailer.

"OHmyGod. That was sooooo funny. At first I thought it was Lena because of the necklace, yaknow cuz of like the close-up but you like swished your face away so I wasn't totally sure who it was but then I thought about it and I knew that it was you since you have long hair and everything." Carol picked up a strawberry and bit the end of it. My stomach rumbled.

Lena received a dozen phone calls from clients and friends wanting to know if she was the one hanging from the dragon. She was known for wearing the phoenix to special occasions. "Right," I said.

"And when you fell on the guard and you knocked the air out of him, I just about peed laughing that was soooo funny." She giggled.

Days later, after Harold had coaxed Lena into being cordial, she still refused to look at me. I finished cleaning up and went outside.

"What are you doing?" She asked.

"I wanted to talk to you." I stepped next to her.

"Look. One of us needs to be inside in case someone comes by."

"I know but—"

"Either you or me."

"I wanted to say—"

"I guess it'll be me." She started to walk by me. I knew that if I waited, then I'd never have the chance to tell her.

"I'm sorry," I said.

Lena's hand rested on the door latch.

"I'm sorry if I embarrassed you or made you mad or anything like that. I didn't mean to do it. It sort of happened." I twisted a napkin. The paper shred.

"Right," she said.

"I won't do it again," I said. Did I mean this? I didn't know. At that moment, I couldn't stand the fact that Lena wouldn't talk to me. If she didn't like me or we weren't the best of friends then that was fine. I needed her to treat me like she did before.

"Remember the gig in Anaheim?" Lena put her arm against the door.

"Yes," I said.

"They canceled." The gig had been one step higher than the ones we'd worked. One step closer to an A-list.

"I'm sorry."

She looked at me. Her eyes filled. Lena's voice lowered. "The producer saw you on TV." The generators hummed. The refrigerator churned more ice, which crashed into the tray below.

"I'm—"

"Yeah. Right. Whatever. Go see if the director needs anything."

I patted my pockets for a notepad.

“You know what? I’ll do it.” She stepped back and walked to the trailer. She tried to run but her feet were swallowed in the sand making her movement slow and forced. I bit into a crisp lettuce leaf. I called Zachary to see if he was free on Saturday for lunch, I needed someone to talk to. I spent the rest of the week trying not to be in Lena’s way.

Zachary greeted me with a hug that I sorely needed. He glanced around the restaurant and got a slightly disgusted look on his face.

“Very quaint.” Zachary lounged in a white rattan chair. He wore a crisp white shirt and dark blue jeans. Since I had last seen him his hair had bleached in the sun while his skin darkened.

Zachary had chosen this place since it was a new café around the corner from his bungalow. “I heard great things,” he said when he sat down. Even though I wasn’t quite sure about how sincere he was based on his expression. The exterior of the restaurant had been painted a pale yellow. I had walked between the tall windows that lined the front. Oversized white fans dropped down from the ceiling. The interior walls had a bevy of daisies, sunflowers, daffodils, carnations and roses painted behind a faux white picket fence. The room had been decorated with white rattan tables and chairs. Outside, round tables and lounge chairs quickly filled with customers. The waiters and waitresses wore white shirts and pants. In the background John Lee Hooker played. I liked the name of the place, “Sunny Afternoon.”

We talked about Zachary’s latest film and the new director he worked for. “An up-and-comer,” he said. Zachary ordered his second club soda with extra ice and a slice of lime. I remembered Lena commenting that you weren’t from LA unless you ordered something that wasn’t available on the menu.

He asked about my flight and my transition to California. He asked about Lena’s business. I told him about the incident. Even though I was sure he already knew about it. He probably even saw it. I pushed the lettuce leaves around the plate and moved the avocado slices so they formed a happy face then a sad face. He laughed. One good thing—he didn't look away or run away when I told him what had happened. I left out the reasons why I tried to get Jonathan's attention. I implied that I wanted to get into the premiere and figured Jonathan was the person who could get me in.

"That crap happens around here all the time. We even had a reporter who would overtly hit on every other celebrity. He always made the local news with his antics. It always dies away."

"Are you sure?" I hadn't eaten in days. Between the dieting and the worry, I couldn't stomach anything. He said that all of this would pass and Lena would get her clients back.

"This is LA. Next time, consider going out with us instead of trekking out on your own."

"How is everything?" Our waitress, a boy-thin woman, asked.

"Lovely, thank you," Zachary replied. She refilled my iced tea and cleared Zachary's empty plate. He had scarfed down his southern fried steak sandwich. "Now for a different topic," he said. "We know that Lena will be fine, but what about you?" He drank from his soda and bit into ice. No one had bothered to ask me that in so long, I nearly wept. None of this trip had turned out how I had expected. I kept my spirits up by reminding myself that I had been invited out here and that Jonathan needed me.

"I'm fine." Next to us, a woman carried shopping bags from Prada, Gucci, Michael Kors. The woman slipped on super dark oversized sunglasses and paid the check. She left the restaurant and headed to the boutiques across the way. We were in a small community Zachary called Toluca Lake. I didn't remember seeing a lake nearby but whatever.

"I don't believe that." Zachary watched the woman as she walked out. Not in a leering kind of way but more so as if he knew her.

I tried to think of what else to say. “I’m not fine.” I pushed my half-eaten salad away and put my hands in my lap. He leaned back in his chair and looked at me in an, “I have all day” kind of way. I observed the others within the restaurant. All actively engaged in conversations. Two men in crisp white shirts and jeans ordered a bottle of wine, their food barely touched. A young blonde woman wearing sunglasses pushed around soup as if she thought the actions might make it disappear from the bowl. “Zachary. You mentioned you weren’t from here. Why did you move to California?”

“Me?” he smirked. “I was going to change the world. Be the next . . .” he waved his hand. “It doesn’t matter. I came with big dreams, no money, from no town USA. I had never seen a skyscraper let alone a designer bag. And I was seventeen.” Zachary reached over with his fork and speared a chunk of avocado. He sniffed it and then plopped it into his mouth.

He leaned back in his chair. “I graduated from high school and decided I didn’t want to go to college. I wanted to be a star. I hitched rides here. By the time I reached LA, my parents realized I had gone. When I called to tell them where I was, they had reported me missing.” He put his napkin on the table. “I reminded them I was legally an adult. Years later, a couple of bouts nearly homeless, too many nights in spots probably best left unstated, and here I am.”

“Is this what you thought it would be?”

“Am I a star?” He laughed. “LA is never what anyone thinks it will be. It’s not like anyplace else.”

More tables emptied. Stragglers finished the last of their meals and continued with their day. Zachary leaned onto the table. He gave me this look, one I hadn’t seen since I had been dropped off at the airport.

“Lauren, what are you looking for?”

"What?"

"I mean, why are you here?"

"To help Lena—"

"That's not why you're here. Everyone comes out here to find something."

"What can I get you?" Our waitress interrupted. I hadn't even seen her approach our table. Zachary straightened up in his seat. He gave me a caring look that surprised me.

"Just the check," Zachary said. "This isn't what you expected. Is it?" he asked me.

"No." I felt myself blush. I didn't know what I expected anymore.

Zachary pulled out his wallet and placed a few bills onto the table. Another couple got up and left the airy café. "I had a really good time when we hung out." Zachary grabbed a napkin and asked the waitress for a pen.

"Me too," I said. Zachary, Lena and I had hung out a few times after the shoots since I'd come to LA. Zachary made me laugh. He acted serious on the set but as soon as we were officially off-duty he was the first to suggest we head out to dinner or happy hour or a movie. Lena had jumped at the chance. At first I felt like a tag-along but then Zachary had said, *we wouldn't invite you if we didn't want you around.* I picked up my purse and dug out my sunglasses, the ones Lena insisted I buy my first day in town.

"If you want, call me. We should get together again." He handed me his numbers—work, home.

"I would like that," I said.

When we got up to leave, he kissed me on the lips. A light kiss. The kind he'd given to Dianne. I wasn't sure what to do. I looked away and then looked back to see find him smiling at me.

"Can I ask you a question?" I said.

He placed his hand on my lower back and brought me a little closer to him. I looked up to find his eyes locked to mine.

"Do you? I mean . . . I didn't think that I was your type," I said. He looked away for a split second and then put his hand on mine.

"Let's just say I have lots of types." His gaze met mine and then he leaned in and kissed me again.

Chapter 20

Underneath a beach umbrella, a man in ragged clothes held a fan of maps. Tourists stared, fascinated by his faded dirty jeans and stained t-shirt. "Maps to the Stars Homes" said a yellowed sign with the names Bela Lugosi and Mel Gibson scribbled on its edge.

"Five dollars," he said in a monotone.

I approached him with the bill in hand. He gave me the map folded like an accordion. One guy passed, he shook his head. The salesman crumpled my bill into a wad of other bills and continued. "Map to the Stars. Five dollars."

At the bus stop, I tried to unwrap it without making a mess. The cartoonish map detailed the winding streets of Hollywood and West Hollywood, Los Angeles and its suburbs. Numbers clustered different sections. Stars marked where a famous person had lived. Stars in the hills, others twinkled on a street or in La Jolla Beach.

The bus arrived. Plastered on its side was an ad for Pepsi. Faces smiled with soda bottles next to their heads. The bus's brakes squeaked as it stopped. I jumbled the map into my bag. In New Jersey, we rode on buses, trains, trolleys, taxis, cars, and subways. California had this strange bus system that seemed to run once an hour. I heard that hitchhiking would have been faster. I guessed that was why everyone in California drove a car.

The Cali bus's doors opened with the sound of released air. I was immediately chilled by it. The bus driver hunched in his seat and continued to look forward as I placed my coins in the tray. They jingled down the slot.

I went to the back. Passengers looked like they came from someplace else. Most wore uniforms like for a maid or a mechanic or a cook. A man slumped in his seat. His clothes crumpled. He stank like liquor had seeped through his pores and escaped into the stale air. This with an underlying smell of sweet smoke and old vomit moved me to the front of the bus.

I sat down on a new hard green plastic seat. As the bus continued forward, I swayed with the turns and stops. My legs floated above the ground. The driver did not acknowledge passengers getting in or getting out. He moved his foot and shifted the bus into gear. Outside, the ground blended into greys and blacks highlighted with gold. The bus's swaying motion turned the trees and highway into an abstract painting. The more I traveled the state the more I wondered if California consisted of only five- to ten-lane highways. We traveled from one remote bus stop to another, until we reentered the city and even then I don't think we turned down a side street or drove one block into a residential section. Grey and black streets and paved roads guided us.

I needed to see where I sent my letters. I envisioned a movie set with huge domed white buildings enclosed by gates. Guards in towers gave or denied access. People dressed for a party, a circus, a romp through the tundra roamed two-lane streets. They chatted as they stopped in the cafeteria for a bite or searched the building with the big letter A on it, because that's where the latest *Indiana Jones* was filmed. A man in a golf cart honked his horn and cursed at a clown talking to Darth Vader.

The bus turned the corner. I anticipated the grandness of the studio, but what I found was a high rise in the middle of Los Angeles. The ice blue glass building reflected the sun's rays which caused ripples from the heat's shimmer. The effect reminded me of ocean waves. The building towered over its neighbors and stretched through the clouds and into the sky.

I pulled on the cord. At the front of the bus, a sign flashed, "request to stop" and a bell sounded. The driver pulled on a lever and gripped the steering wheel. The bus slowed and then stopped with screeching brakes. With a single arm movement the doors flung open. My feet barely touched the pavement when I heard the doors clunk closed and the brakes release. Pepsi's smiling faces flew past.

Pedestrians strolled by. The air grew still. Across the way, a high rise with "Goliath Incorporated" scripted on the doors. The building grew from the pavement with stories too numerous to count. It disappeared into the sky.

I entered through the main entrance, which floated in silvers and blues. The opaque walls allowed me to see the blurs of people. The hall contained a guard desk and across the way waited an elevator encapsulated in black marble. Tourists preoccupied the security guard as they tried to take pictures with him. I jumped into the elevator, with a rise in my chest. The door sealed shut behind me. A wall of buttons glowed with my touch. I pressed the number for the studio.

With a low ding we reached the thirty-third floor. The elevator hushed to a stop. The doors slid open to reveal a bright white hallway with indirect lights on the ceiling, which caused everything to glow. For a moment, I wondered if I'd walked onto a set for the movie *Oh, God! Part III.*

I ducked into a hall bathroom. The small white room sterile with only a toilet, a sink, and a mirrored medicine cabinet. I smelled like I had worn my jeans for days and my hair looked like a cat's fur ball. The tap water ran cool against my skin. The water shushed as it gurgled down the drain. I soaked paper towels and rinsed off my face and arms. I looked in the mirror, still bothered by my own smell. I opened my backpack and searched for a small bottle of perfume. I felt around and palmed something the right size and shape. When I pulled it out, Nuri's bottle tumbled to the ground. It cracked against the tile floor. I scooped it up and tucked it back into the bag. I put my stray hairs into place and took out the package I needed to deliver. I had told Zach that I'd meet him this night for dinner. I needed to get this done.

At the desk, an older woman dressed in a pale tan pants suit answered phones. Her pinned up silver hair looked fluffy compared to her facial features. Her face taut and shiny like a porcelain doll's. Her suit blended so well with her skin that at first she looked naked and without shadows or variations in tone. Even her hair and makeup were pale tones of tan and white, which combined with the indirect light, made her look unearthly.

"May I help you?"

"Where does the mail go once it's sent here?" I asked.

"Do you have an appointment?" She smiled.

"I'm sorry? I wanted to know what happens to the mail once it's sent here. It's important."

She snickered. "I'm sure it is but I need to know if you have an appointment before I can answer that question."

I deliberated what to say. I placed the package on top of the reception area and tapped it with my fingers.

"Are you delivering that package, Miss?" She asked. Not wanting to miss my opportunity, I started to explain about the mail that I had sent. She listened and nodded. "You want to know what happens to the mail once it leaves here."

I agreed.

"That's not a simple answer. But for our purposes, let's say that there is an enormous mail bin in the back and everything is sorted there. Then, all the mail is sent to each addressee's homes or wherever designated. Does that help?"

"I guess."

"If you want, I will take that package by hand to the back room and make sure that it is put in the proper space for Mr. Pearce." She reached out and moved the package towards her.

"Is there any way I can have his address? I'll deliver it." I shifted my backpack from one arm to the other. It felt heavier the longer I held it. I glanced at my watch. If I hurried, I probably had enough time to get this done and meet Zach. I may have to ask him to meet me a little later. He wouldn't mind. At least I hoped he wouldn't.

She looked at me from the tops of her glasses. "Now you and I both know that's not going to happen. You are more than welcome to write a note to Mr. Pearce asking for his address. I'll be sure to give it to him." Her fingernails clicked against the keyboard.

I had made it difficult for him to get in touch with me. What was I thinking? I should have sent him my new phone number and address before I stepped foot in this state. Her suggestion might be better.

"May I have a pen and paper?" She handed me a white plastic pen and a clear clipboard. I nestled into a metal chair, hidden in a corner. I wrote and rewrote what I wanted to say. Visitors came in and out from behind the reception area.

I sealed the note, careful to make sure it was tightly closed and placed it in the package. The receptionist looked up when I approached her desk. She acknowledged it and then disappeared into the back. Moments later, she reappeared and took her spot behind the desk.

"He'll be sure to get it?" I asked.

"He'll be sure to get it." She nodded and returned to answering phones.

Something wasn't right. I don't know if it was her stance or how she responded or the fact that she turned away so quickly but I knew she was hiding something from me.

"Is there anything else?" she asked.

She said Jonathan got the letters but how could I be sure? I knew he wanted to talk to me so why wouldn't he write back? "How do I know?"

She pushed a button on the switchboard. It flashed and glowed red. "We already discussed that. I'll be sure it gets to the proper place."

Behind her appeared a tanned man in a dark suit. He materialized through the wall. "Lou. I believe this young lady is lost and needs someone to show her the way out."

"How do I know?" I should have stopped asking. I should have thanked her and left without a single question, but I couldn't do it. I needed to know.

"Miss. I'll be happy to escort you to the elevators." The man floated around the receptionist area, his presence a stark contrast to everything else in the room. The lines of his suit looked harsh against the glowing light. I knew they wanted to get rid of me. Who did they think they were dealing with? Some child?

I knew Jonathan never got a single letter. He had no idea I had been waiting for him. Every single note I had ever written had been piled in the back.

I scouted the clearest path between the receptionist and the suited man, then dashed through the clearing and leapt for the back room. I scanned the area for the letters, our letters. Sure to stay down and try to stay out of sight, I eyed every nook and cranny in anticipation of finding them.

I knew better than to look behind me. If I even wavered for a second, he'd catch me. He tailed me by a fraction of an inch, his fingertips touched the back of my shirt. Before me beaconed a doorway previously hidden in the stark white walls. I reached for the frame. If I grabbed it then I could pull into the back room and slam the door behind me and escape.

"I don't think—" He yanked my shirt and took me off my feet. Stalled me in mid-stride. His balled fist contained a good section of my shirt, my stomach exposed. I dangled there and churned to break free.

"You don't fool me!" I flung my arms around and jammed my backpack at his head. I kicked behind me in the hopes that I'd hit his shin or knee or something that would make him scream out in pain and set me free.

He didn't say a word but instead wrenched my hands behind my back so I couldn't thrash against him. He shoved my arm back with such force that pain shot through my shoulders, my arms became useless. My legs flailed in the air trying to push against something, anything to help me.

"I'm not done yet!" I screamed. "What *makes* you *think* this is *right*?"

The receptionist's once motherly demeanor now looked on with dark shadows under her eyes and cheekbones. Her sharpened teeth protruded into a grin.

"I think you are," she hissed.

He threw me into a side elevator. I bounced off the back. The walls and ceiling lined in soiled dark brown padding. I crumpled on the bottom. Moments later the freezing metal floor jarred me awake. I tested my arms and legs to make sure everything worked. My backpack landed next to me in a jumble. At least I still had it. The earth shifted beneath me. I floated above the coldness until a screeching noise announced that the elevator was about to stop and my body reconnected with the ground. The doors behind me flew open to reveal an alley. I needed to get back inside. I grabbed my bag and ran to the front of the building. At the main door three security guards in black suits blocked the entry.

I paced the street. I noted their hardened faces. Their lack of emotion. This kept my words from coming out. I nodded, took a deep breath, and strolled around the building. I needed to find another way in. The elevator doors sealed against me. I could only get in by the front door.

I fumbled with my door key. After a few attempts, it jerked open. I could barely move from the pain. The trip back to the apartment gave my aches a chance to catch up with me. Lena lounged in the kitchenette, a cigarette dangling from her fingers. She blew a halo of smoke out the window.

"What happened to you now?" She searched in the alcove under the cabinets to find a first aid kit. I prayed I would make it to the couch. I wanted to crawl onto the rug and fall asleep. The scratches, cuts, and blotchy bruises rose up from my skin.

"I fell," I said.

"Yeah right. Fell." Before I made it to the couch, she held my hand and led me to the bathroom. Lena eased me onto the toilet seat, my knees barely able to bend. She cleansed and covered the sores in antiseptic and creams. The smells stung my nose and the fluid burned the scratches. Then she smeared on a cooling salve.

She didn't say much. I couldn't speak. I was afraid of what she might say. In the silence, I thought of what I could say or should say. When she finished, I was layered in antiseptic, salve and band aids. She backed onto the rim of the tub.

"Now give. What happened and don't try that 'I fell' story."

The bandages turned different shades of pink. The color spread across the fresh cotton.

She shook her head and stood up, a cigarette at the ready. I got up and tried to think of an explanation she would accept. She went into the main room and then the kitchen and lit a cigarette off the gas stove. Through the hallway I watched as the tip of her cigarette glowed and she let out a sigh with her first exhale.

I stopped at the couch. I started to tell her what had happened. Note the "started to." I got as far as the guy in the suit showing up behind the receptionist when . . .

"I thought you had more sense than that?" Lena blew a puff of smoke through her nostrils.

"I—"

"Didn't working on an A-list movie teach you better?" She picked a piece of tobacco from her lip. "Lauren, they don't care about you. They don't care about anyone but themselves."

"That's not true." I whispered. "He loves me."

"Loves you? Lauren, he can't love you." Lena pulled on her cigarette. She inhaled half of it. One of her hands clasped the stub, the other pointed out all I had missed. "Those movie stars don't care about you. Didn't you learn that? All they do is act nice and tell people how much they love them. It isn't real."

Her words stung more than the scratches. Her fingertips burned on the ash. "Fuck." She tossed the stub into the sink and drowned it in water. She caught her breath and watched the cigarette end spiral down the drain. She put her hands through her hair. And then the doorbell rang. Zach. Crap, I had forgotten about Zach. Lena answered the door. "What are you doing here?"

"Lauren and I—Jesus. What happened to you?" Zach sat next to me on the couch, his hands hovering over the bandages as if he was afraid to touch me.

"I fell?" I said. I couldn't look at Zach. I didn't dare look at Lena.

"You know what? That's it. This is all you. You wanna believe whatever you wanna believe. Don't come to me when he doesn't remember your name." She picked up her bag and headed for the door and slammed it behind her.

The remnants of Lena's anger stayed with me. I looked up at the ceiling. My mind fixed on what had to be true.

“What’s she talking about?” Zach asked.

“Nothing,” I said. “Just . . . nothing.” I kissed Zach on the cheek and snuggled against him. “Let’s go out. Or even stay in? Just go somewhere other than here.”

Chapter 21

Zachary took me out for a vanilla milkshake and a cheeseburger at In-N-Out. "You need comfort food," he said. We talked away the night. I felt so at ease with him, in a way I hadn't imagined before. He made me laugh so hard I nearly snorted. Turns out his latest boss was great at getting into even more elaborate antics than mine. And he asked me lots of questions and politely avoided asking about what had happened. I guess my nonverbal signals let him know that I wouldn't have answered them anyway. We talked for so long that missed the movie. I didn't mind. We went back to his place for a bit. By the time I got home, the wear and tear of the day finally hit me. I barely made it to my bed.

My dreams filled with the images of Jonathan. He came out of his home and greeted me. Welcomed me home. He hugged me, protected me from the pains of the last month. "Lovely," he said and kissed the scrapes on my face and my bandaged hands. I never felt so secure. The odd part was his scent. He didn't smell like the musky cologne he'd worn before but like Ivory soap, hair gel, and men's musky deodorant. And he didn't sound like Jonathan either. I awoke and shook away the sleep. A sense of calmness and rightness stayed. I didn't dare see if Lena had returned.

I didn't want to hurt Lena or make her feel obligated. Besides, she'd see me as soon as she got back. The day after I had arrived, I had put in for the available studio. I couldn't believe how long it was taking for the lease to go through. I decided it was time to bug the super about it. After some negotiating the super gave me a key to a different studio. "It was reserved for someone else," he said. "But your check cleared first so it's yours. Although," he continued. He hovered the key over my hand. "I didn't finish the background check." Based on where we lived I was surprised he even did one. He dropped the key into my hand. "I suppose it's fine."

I didn't have much to take with me. Only the boxes that I mailed to myself and two pieces of luggage. I stacked them in front of the door to my temporary new home. The door squeaked open and revealed a studio apartment smaller than Lena's place. I nudged the boxes inside. The kitchenette had only two burners on the stove top and a mini fridge crammed underneath the counter. To the right of the doorway was a bathroom with a shower stall, sink, and toilet. I had to squeeze by the toilet to get to the shower but that was fine. Enough room for one person. Some closets were bigger than this place. I knew I wouldn't live here long.

I bought a cot from the Army and Navy store and put it in a corner to double as a couch. At Goodwill I bought sheets and a comforter along with framed pictures of flowers and children playing. I figured they'd make the apartment feel homey.

Lena didn't comment about the move. When I gave her the studio number, she seemed relieved to have her place to herself. Zach didn't question it. If anything he seemed happy about the change. Lena knocked on my door and peered inside. "Are you ready?" she asked. We had another on location shoot. I grabbed a light jacket since the filming might last late into the night. I followed her to the truck. She barely acknowledged me. The silence brought back the humiliation of our fight. I got into the truck with only the sound of the closing door. I folded my hands in my lap.

Lena looked at the road ahead. The engine grinded as she turned the key. She mumbled something and tried again. The churning seemed to go on for hours. I wanted to say something to make this easier, less stressful, but I couldn't think of anything. She rested her head against the steering wheel and closed her eyes. After a moment, she reached over and turned the key again. This time the engine puttered and then caught. I wiggled in my seat, to find a comfortable position over the coil.

Daylight wouldn't come for a little while. I wished for the hazy colors of the morning. At least it would mean we were further along in the day. I put my arm against the window frame, trying to feel at ease. The smell of engine oil came from the vents. I hoped we didn't need to walk soon.

As we continued onward, the signs of morning came through the windows. Birds on telephone wires. More cars on the road. The haze of morning coming over the horizon. On the way to the site, an orange orchard a few hours away from our complex, Lena started to speak to me again. "How you like your new digs?"

"They're fine," I said.

She lit a cigarette and tapped the tip off through the window. The ashes evaporated in the air. "Need anything?" She played with the radio dial.

"I don't think so." I nodded and crossed my arms. She glanced at me and then she turned up the music. The Ramones' "I Wanna Be Sedated" came through the speakers.

Chapter 22

She left his house. I followed her to the corner, where the bus stop had been marked by a lone sign and a glass enclosure riddled with graffiti.

She had changed out of her uniform and into jeans and a red shirt. The oversized shirt covered her body shape and stopped at the top of her knees. Her jet-black hair had been pulled back into a bun. She looked so young. Her hair severe against her unmarked face.

I wondered if she had started working as a teenager, like me. I waited next to her. We were almost the same height. I may have been a half-inch taller, if that. Dark liquid lines circled her large brown eyes. Her slightly chapped full lips had been tinted with red. In one hand she clutched an oversized purse, a Chanel rip-off. In the other she rolled coins between her fingers. She didn't smell of food, like I thought she would. All the years I worked at the diner, I smelled of the Ps' daily special whether I wanted to or not. She smelled clean.

"Excuse me," I said. She looked at me for a second. "I don't mean to disturb you but how much is this bus? I'm trying to get to . . ." I named the last location on the schedule.

She squinted her eyes and rolled her neck. "Why, you don't know?"

"I'm sorry. I just started working around the corner at the big yellow mansion."

"You 'elping Marisa?"

"Yes, Marisa. At the Gandolfino's." That's the name that was on their mail.

Her face softened. "Good. Good. She need help. Too many chil'ren in that house." The bus stopped before us. I followed her onto it. "What you doing for Marisa?"

"Whatever she needs," I said. She smiled at that. "Where do you work?" I asked her. She sat in the aisle across from me, clear that she didn't want someone next to her. I nestled across from her on the half empty bus. The vehicle shushed as it accelerated, jerking with the exertion.

"At Mr. Pearce's home." She grabbed the handrail and steadied as we hedged forward.

"I thought I saw him down the street," I said. I glanced out of the window to hide a smile.

"Mus' be someone else. He no home." She looked a little surprised at what she said, then she looked at me.

"It must be boring without him around," I said, sure to say this with concern.

She shifted in her seat and straightened her back. "Nono. We fine. We do our thing whether he there or not."

The bus stopped. An older man got off and a young girl with headphones got on. As she passed us I heard the beat from Michael Jackson's "Thriller" coming from the music player. The cook reached into her purse and pulled out a soft ginger candy.

"I love those. They're the best," I said.

"You know these?" she asked. "My auntie used to buy them for me. That was our Sunday treat."

"My grandma bought these for us. Sundays too," I said. She smiled and offered me a candy.

"Thank you," I said.

"Here—here." She handed it to me. "To familia."

I unwrapped the sweet and spicy candy and popped it into my mouth. I silently chewed.

"I'm Betsy," I said.

"Adrianna. Nice to meet you. You 'elp Marisa long?" she asked. The bus felt like it would topple over as we turned a corner. I gripped the rail before me, my knuckles turned white. My butt rose off the seat.

"Only a couple of days. Then I go back to my regular client."

"Si, si. They always moving us around."

"Yes." I swallowed the last of the candy. "What do you do when he's not around?"

"You kidding?" She turned to me and adjusted her purse on her lap. "We cook for Murial and Jose and Josephine and everybody. Not as busy but still busy. I get house ready for when he come back. He always have red and white wine, fruit and those stinky cheeses when he home."

The bus driver called out the next stop.

"That me. Say 'hola' to Marisa for me. I see her at de market."

I nodded and watched as she left. She ambled down a street filled with small ranchers that looked more like shacks. In front of the corner house a car covered in rust had been propped on cement blocks. The bus continued forward.

At home, I pulled out my latest journal to capture every moment. I had filled books with clippings and notes. I remarked on how one of the maids always arrived late. How Adrianna put out the trash after every meal and wore clear plastic gloves. When the mail was delivered and what the mailman looked like (tubby man, balding with peeling sunburn).

I stored the journals in my closet. At night I reviewed them to see if I missed anything. Any commonalities or bits of information. I snuck over to his house when we weren't working. Careful to avoid questions that Lena or Zach may have. I had learned from the last several months. I had made too many mistakes. At least I knew better than to mention these activities to Zach. He definitely wouldn't like it. We had been spending so much time together, at least when he was in town. He still traveled a lot for work, which was fine. It gave me more time on my own.

I must admit, I wasn't sure what I was doing with Zach. He seemed to want so much. Every time we were together he talked like we were in it for the long term. He even hinted at moving in together. "Not yet," I had said. I didn't want to lose him. Something about him made me happy. He was a great blend of best friend and lover. Never in a million years would I have guessed that we would be together. Part of me needed him around but then there was the other part, the part that needed to be near Jonathan. The part that haunted in the middle of the night. The part that needed to know about Jonathan's life and knew, just knew that she was meant to be in it. The part that called herself Betsy to those who worked for him.

After I read the clippings and looked at the maps, photos and such, I felt the box beneath my bed call to me. I caressed the lid and held it to my chest. Soon, I thought.

Chapter 23

The map fluttered in the Santa Ana winds. I gripped the page tighter. I stood at the trolley stop, the one next to Mann's Chinese Theatre. Every half-hour a new trolley came. I only needed patience. Tourists filled the trolley stop. Their cameras hung from their necks and sunblock coated their skin.

I didn't care what Goliath Studios' secretary said or what Lena claimed. They couldn't stop me from seeing Jonathan. He wanted me there. The trolley looked exactly like something out of a Rice-a-Roni commercial. It approached the stop with the same ring-a-ling the closer it came. The driver's angular face was partially masked by a trolley captain's hat. His dark hair clumped in oily tangles that licked the back of his neck. He looked at me through the hat's bill. He wore a navy suit with a white and gold emblem, a trolley with wings on its breast pocket. He wordlessly directed me to the back.

The wooden seats reminded me of park benches with poles interspersing each section. The open windows allowed the summery breeze in. "Thanks," I said and chose the seat directly behind him.

He turned to me. "Not there," he clipped. The next customer came onto the trolley, hand full of money. "I save that seat for the handicapped."

"Oh. Sorry." I got up and moved two seats away from him.

Three more tourists paid their fares and took their spots. After the last one sat down, the driver stomped on the clutch, which jerked the trolley forward. He pushed play on a tape recorder underneath a microphone. Both were adhered to the dashboard with silver duct tape edged in old globs of adhesive, which balled in the sides where the tape had curled. The voice of Marilyn Monroe said, "Please keep your limbs in the trolley at all times." John Wayne continued, "Don't leave the trolley unless you're told to do it by the operator, pardner." The tourists laughed. I took out my map again. I got up and inched back behind the trolley driver. The recording continued to tell us about the streets and homes. The trolley turned and followed the previously prepared route. I compared my map to the neighborhoods and the trolley route to the regular bus. I thought this would be the better approach. Not as conspicuous. The trolley moved slower than a bus, which made the narrow roads and houses easier to see.

"Excuse me?" I said.

He ignored me.

"Excuse me? Sir?" I tapped him on the shoulder.

"Do not bother the trolley driver while we are in motion," he said.

I tried not to scream. I slowed my breathing and tried again when we stopped at the red light. "Excuse me. Will we stop at Jonathan Pearce's house?"

"We'll go by all the stars' houses," he said.

"Great. When will we stop at his home?"

"That's the deluxe tour. This is the standard tour. If you want the deluxe tour then you have to pay for it."

I should have guessed. I sucked my teeth. "Fine. How much for the deluxe tour?" I took my money from my pocket. He looked at me through the rear mirror, he skimmed my clothes and what I carried. I hid my cash inside my jeans.

"Twenty bucks more," he said.

"Twenty bucks? The standard tour is only fifteen dollars." The trolley jerked forward. I almost fell head first into the front window.

"Behind the line please." He pointed below at a yellow line my foot had crossed. "You're the one who wants the stop."

"Fine. Great. Here." I handed him the twenty and watched it disappear into his jacket.

"When we get to his house, I'll stop the trolley."

I wanted to grab the twenty dollars and tell him where to stick it. I reached forward only inches from his coat pocket and then I retracted it. I sat back in my seat and fidgeted while I waited for his hand motion or a look to let me know when it was safe to get off.

We passed homes of stars from the 1940s and 1950s, then he pointed out David Hasselhoff's mansion, another owned by Madonna, a third had been used in *Sixteen Candles.* I shifted in my seat and tried to remain calm. Stay patient. The trolley turned a corner. This took too long. The white mansion with black iron gating arose from the street. The operator nodded to the house. I waited for the trolley to slow down, at least a little. He didn't. Instead, he sped up.

"I'm getting off." I jumped from my seat.

"I don't think so. Listen to Mr. Wayne." He pressed start on the recorder and John Wayne's voice returned. The driver thrust his foot on the accelerator. The trolley continued ahead. Passengers held onto the rails to keep from falling. Their bags slid across the floor.

I clutched one handrail to another until I reached the front door. I stood at the bottom step and pushed at the door.

"What do you think you're doing?" he cried. I looked back; his fist came dangerously close to me.

"I'm going where I need to be." I shoved against the doors with my shoulder. The trolley slowed and I jammed with the rest of my weight. Then impact. I took a breath and then I rolled onto the street, hugged my bag to my chest, and rolled away from the vehicle. Horns honked and voices cursed. "What are you crazy?" Someone called from a passing car.

"Freakin' nut!" The driver yelled. Good thing I watched *Stuntman TV*. The tourists' cameras clicked away. Then the tourists clapped.

I rolled to the sidewalk's edge and lay there for a moment. I hadn't planned on jumping from the trolley. I really didn't. But I was forced to do it. Wasn't that obvious? So much for blending in. I didn't want to look at the state of my clothes or check on my bruises. I could tell from the pain that there would be more than I wanted to count. Even more than I could acknowledge. I didn't want to be preoccupied with minor things like that when I had something to finish. Zach kept talking about moving in together, about long term things. I had been putting him off for what felt like months. I couldn't make a commitment to him until this was done.

I moved my fingers and toes, then my wrists and ankles, and then my elbows and knees. I felt my arms and legs for breaks. I had sore spots but nothing resembled a broken bone. I edged my way onto the curb. I touched my face. It had been seared with scrapes. I opened my backpack and removed a tissue to dab at the rough spots. The cloth became spotted with blood. There wasn't enough blood to be worried about but more than enough to know that Lena would have a fit when she saw me. My sneakers had been torn and scuffed. I looked up to see the two-lane street and the white mansion circled by black ironwork. The gating's collage had birds soaring to their destiny. I imagined flying with them, through the clouds and closer to the sun.

I made my way to the main gate and pressed the glowing button on the black intercom. A camera turned. It peered at me.

I touched the camera, curious how it worked. "Hello?" I asked.

"Yes." An older man's voice crackled through the tinny speaker.

"I have a delivery." I put my bag in front of the lens. The intercom clicked.

"No deliveries today."

"I'm a day early," I said.

Click. "Come back when you are scheduled." The glow on the intercom faded, the camera's whirring stopped. The driveway empty.

I waved at the intercom and headed back to the street. The camera's lens followed me. Well, that didn't work. I adjusted my jeans. The knee had been torn out, my shirtsleeve ripped and stained from the asphalt. My arms and legs dotted in scratches and bruises.

I wandered around the outside of the house. A cement block wall had been painted white to match the mansion. Other than small decorative squares along the wall's top, no other openings revealed the home's contents. On the side, another black iron gate with a similar bird theme guarded the place. An entrance used by the servants remained closer to the back. Trashcans lined the inside wall. Beyond them was a door to what looked like the kitchen. A shadow moved within and peered out.

Chapter 24

The door slid open. "Hello? Marisa need something?" Adrianna opened the door wider. She wore an apron with black piping, a white button-down shirt, and pristine black pants. "What 'appen to you? Come, come."

I followed her inside. The kitchen must have been twice the size of my old home. In the center, a long white and grey marble aisle anchored the room. Two sinks with curving water fixtures sunk within it. Windows filled the room with soft light. White cabinets with golden knobs lined the walls to the left. To the right, a half-wall slightly dipped to an open room filled with soft white leather furniture and modern paintings. It looked just like the photos in *American Home.*

A golden winding staircase curved to the second floor where a walkway balanced above. Beyond the rooms were more windows and a grand garden even more impressive than those on *Home and Garden TV.* In the middle of the yard was a pool the shape of two connected circles.

"Come, come," she said. Her face, clean of makeup, looked even younger than she did before. I silently followed her to a kitchen sink the size of a child's bathtub. She turned on the faucet and water rushed from the golden fixtures. It splashed into the marble below and swirled down the drain.

Now that Adrianna pointed them out to me, my sores oozed. My skin on fire from the welts. I looked at my arms and legs and could have screamed. My pants were ripped at the knees. Random tears ran throughout the cloth. Telltale signs of blood soaked the material. The cool air of the house breathed onto the scratches making them burn.

She took a washcloth and ran it under the water. She held her hand under the tap, adjusted the knobs and shook her head. "This fine," she murmured. She stopped up the sink and allowed the water to pool and then shut off the flow. "I'll be back. Stay here." She went down the hall and into a side door, returning a moment later with a counter stool in one hand and creams in the other. "You sit."

I obeyed. My bones began to ache. My head pounded. I repeatedly looked to the doorway and hoped to see Jonathan. He should be back soon. My arm raged with fire. I jerked it back.

"Sorry. You gots dirt in these." She had taken a washcloth and started cleaning out the scratches. I tried to smile but it was hard. "'ere, take these." She gave me a handful of aspirin. "They take the sting away." She looked at my face and then the sores. "You want Marisa to come get you?"

"No," I said a little too rushed. "I'll be fine. You don't have to clean me up. See?" I raised an arm and wiggled my fingers.

"Ay Dios mío. Gringa es loca," she mumbled.

"I'm sorry?"

"Nothing."

On the counter was a wooden board with cheeses and slices of apples and pears. Two bottles, one white and one red, chilled in black marble coolers. The bottles frosted from the ice.

"May I use the bathroom?" I asked.

She finished cleaning one of the cuts and said, "Go ahead. Use that one there." She nodded to the doorway. I eased off the stool and walked into the bathroom. Sitting gave my body time to register the pain. I could barely move without screaming. I clutched the edge of the center aisle to keep my balance. This isn't quite what I thought would happen. I closed the door behind me and turned on the light.

The bathroom had mirrors for walls and white fixtures with golden accents. My reflection went on forever, getting smaller and smaller. I didn't recognize myself. A human blob of cuts, scratches and smears of blood. Only one arm looked almost human. The pain even greater. I thunked down onto the toilet. I needed to lay down but decided not to. I rested my head in my hands to push the headache and the searing away. *Why was I doing this again? Was this worth it? After so much time, he had to still want me, right?* I couldn't have been totally wrong about this. I couldn't have misunderstood the signs. He asked me out. He kissed me. He said he loved me.

I felt through my bag and found the blue bottle. It twinkled. I searched for the piece of paper. It had stuck in the bag's folds. I read the saying three times as I uncorked and drank the bottle's contents. I didn't pay attention to the taste. I was too busy hoping it would help. I slipped to the floor, my back against the sink and rested. All I wanted was rest.

"Lauren?" His voice. "Are you okay?" I opened my eyes. Jonathan kneeled before me. "My God. What happened to you?" He lifted his hand to touch my cheek.

"I'll be fine," I croaked. He touched my face with the tips of his fingers, feeling the sensitive skin. Even a feather touch felt like a slap. I jerked away from him.

"I'm sorry. It's just . . ." I started.

He moved his arm under my lower back, then nudged his other arm underneath the crook of my legs and lifted me up. Pain raced through my body. I curved against him and the pain dissipated. He hugged me to him and brushed his lips against my forehead. I hid my face in his shirt. The soft cotton warmed from his body.

We floated out of the bathroom. My eyes closed against him. I'm not sure where he took me. We lifted higher and higher. I clutched my hands around his neck, sure not to leave him.

"I'm going to set you down," he said. I saw the man I fell in love with. The one with the purest heart. The one who made the pain go away.

My hands loosened around his neck as he gently placed me down on the soft surface. I opened my eyes. I curled on the edge of a large round bed. I lay on top of the softest down comforter I had ever felt. I melted into it. I snuggled my face into the pillow. I couldn't imagine moving.

He left and returned a moment later. He had a bottle similar to the one Nuri had given me. He rested next to me and uncorked the bottle. He poured the contents into his palm and rubbed it against my face. My skin became cool, the angry sores tamed. He took another fingerful and continued to rub it against my skin until he had covered every angry scratch and scrape. I felt light, tingly, like I floated above the bed. I must have fallen asleep because when I opened my eyes I was underneath the comforter, my ruined clothes removed.

The bedroom contained the bed and a TV that filled the opposite wall. A door framed each end of the TV set. To the left was the door that must have led to the hallway. The other an entry to the bathroom. A wall of windows to the right. Light seeped in bringing particles of sparkling dust. Beyond the windows were clouds, sky, and ocean. All blues and whites, calm, clean, and heaven.

Jonathan entered from the door to the right of the TV. He brought in the tray of cheeses and wine. "Oh good. You're awake," he said. "How do you feel?"

I looked around the room to make sure he was talking to me. When I was certain that we were alone, I hesitated and then said, "Great."

"Good. Now sit up. I thought we could share."

I propped against the round oversized pillows. My muscles ached from the movement. He placed the bamboo tray on the bed and poured us each a glass.

His white cotton shirt and pants were slightly creased and crinkled from wear. His shirt opened to reveal his collarbone and the glimmer of a golden chain. His bare feet hung over the bed's edge. I wanted to lean in and touch him but I waited, I hesitated. This had been so long in coming.

He handed me a glass of the amber drink. He sipped from his own glass and looked at me. I looked away. He held a piece of cheese and took a bite, then took my chin in his hand and turned my head toward him. Then he plopped the rest of the cheese into my mouth. His fingertips brushed my lips. I enjoyed the sharp taste.

"You must be famished," he said.

"I guess . . ."

He kissed the curve of my lip. I felt his breath against my skin with each word. "I missed you." He whispered in my ear. His hand followed the back of my neck and undid the rubber band. My hair fell in waves and covered my eyes. The tips touched the ends of my nipples. With his pointer finger he brushed the hair away and then he started to kiss from the tip of my earlobe, along my jaw line, to the curve of my mouth and then I tasted him. My hands followed his arms and felt the curve of his muscles. I sought the buttons of his shirt. I fumbled to undo them. In the kiss he laughed and helped me to release him from his clothes. A jumble of effort until we were both under the covers.

I followed the definition of his chest, the lines around his hipbones, played with his hair, felt him. His kisses left my mouth and went down my throat to my collarbone to my breasts and created a path where he began to play. He played there for what felt like an eternity. My body shook. He joined me. I wanted to cry out. My body and mind filled with it.

I closed my eyes while lost in the feeling. The pink and swirls of my eyelids grew darker then black. Pitch. I couldn't feel him anymore. I couldn't sense him. What did I do? I felt for him. No, this couldn't be right. He wanted me. He loved me. He couldn't have gone away. I opened my eyes but all I found was darkness. He couldn't have left. He couldn't have. I felt for some sign of him. Something that told me he was still there.

"Lauren?" His voice different somehow. Tense, confused.

"Jonathan?" The room still dark. I felt around the bed. I only found tangled sheets.

"Is that you?" Not his voice.

I stopped moving, my nakedness raw. I searched for the comforter to cover me. I grabbed it and tossed it around me, terrified that I had been seen.

"Oh my God. That is you. What are you doing here?" Her voice became shrill. The black turned to grey. I rubbed my eyes. A blur of a woman only yards away from me. Her outline came into focus.

"Dianne?" I said.

Dianne and Jonathan stood in the doorway.

"How the hell did you get in here?" Jonathan asked.

"I'm supposed to be here." I clutched the covers closer to me. I searched the room, which suddenly felt foreign. I looked down to see them holding hands. Oh my God, they held hands. I didn't understand. The rumors of them being together couldn't have been true. How could he be with her when he was with me?

"I don't think so." He searched the pockets of his black jeans and then his black t-shirt. I wanted to hide under the bed. Instead I cocooned myself into the comforter even more.

"Lauren, why are you here?" Dianne asked.

"How did you get in here?" Jonathan asked.

I didn't know what to say. This wasn't how I had imagined it. He was supposed to be alone. He had been alone with me but then somehow Dianne got here. None of this made sense. *You wanted me, right? How did she get here?*

"Did someone let you in?" Dianne continued. When I didn't answer because I simply didn't know how to answer, she said, "I think we need to make a call." Her red dress and heels blared against the white room.

I hurriedly got out of the bed and searched for my clothes. I looked behind the dresser and under the bed. I did my best not to look at either of them. I needed to get out of there and clear my head. Too much confusion. Too many things that didn't make sense.

"What are you doing here?" asked Dianne. "You're supposed to be in New Jersey."

I looked behind the television, even behind the curtains.

With her words I found the courage to say, "You invited me." I looked up at Jonathan to see his face contort in disgust. "Didn't you?"

"You're going to get out. That's what you're going to do." Jonathan picked up the gold and white phone. He started to dial and then put the phone down. He called for Adrianna.

I had been skipping my visits into the hills. I missed my morning runs. The other day, Zachary called. He had gotten back into town after a shoot in London. He wanted to see me. He *needed* to see me, he had said.

"Now Jonathan, don't you think—" Dianne started.

"Hello," Zachary had said. I melted into the couch and curled my knees up to my chest. "Takeout?" Zachary had asked. I smiled. "Sure."

"Stay out of it Dianne," Jonathan said. "Go on. Get those on." He pointed at my clothes crumbled in a corner. I grabbed them and sprinted for the bathroom. Behind him came Adrianna. "Yes, Mr. Pearce."

Zachary had taken me to the one-dollar movie theater. We ordered buttered popcorn, the bag between us. We watched the original *Sabrina*, the one where Humphrey Bogart turned to Audrey Hepburn and began to declare his love. That's when Zachary moved the bag of popcorn, took my face in his hands and caressed my jaw with his thumb. He grazed his lips against mine and then his kisses went deeper. I responded in a way I didn't expect. We missed the rest of the movie. I awoke the next morning in Zachary's shirt. He turned to me and asked me again. "Move in with me." I knew I had to find out if Jonathan really wanted me.

In the bathroom I turned on the spigot and scrubbed my hands and face, anything to get this grime off of me. I held back the need to cry. I didn't want to put those clothes back on. I wanted to somehow be transported to Zachary. I wanted him to say what he tried to tell me the other night.

"Not yet," I had told him.

"What do you mean, 'not yet?'" Zachary had stepped back.

"I need to figure something out," I had said.

"Even after all this?" Zachary grabbed his jacket and headed for the door. "By now I thought you would have learned something." He opened the door.

I had huddled in the stillness of my studio after he left. He didn't call. Not the next day. Nor the next.

I pulled on my clothes heavy with dirt and guilt. I came out of the bathroom, my head down. "I'm sorry. I'll leave." I zipped past Dianne and Jonathan and nearly knocked Adrianna over. "What you doing here, Betsy?" she asked. "I thought you gone."

"Betsy? Who's Betsy?" Jonathan followed me.

I ran down the steps. I prayed that I could catch Zachary tonight. I prayed it wasn't too late. I scurried through the downstairs and spotted my backpack near the end of the hallway. I jumped the last step and reached for my bag. I glanced behind me to see Adrianna nearby looking confused. "I'll tell Marisa you miss her." I tossed on my backpack and the contents flew across the room. I scrambled to pick them up.

"What's this?" Jonathan picked up the black comb. "I've been looking for this."

I froze. I had forgotten about it.

"Did you steal that?" he asked.

"No," I blurted. "I found it on the set in Jersey. Thought I should return it."

I dropped the backpack onto the floor.

"What? Another freakin' nutcase," said Jonathan. "This is what I get for being nice."

"Adrianna, I'll tell Marisa to call you later," I said. I ran for the back door and pushed it open.

I waited in front of Zachary's for what felt like an eternity. His small bungalow locked up tight except for a light he had hooked up to an auto timer. It flickered on as the evening fell. He couldn't have left LA already.

To be honest, I'm not sure how I made it to Zach's in one piece. I had raced down Jonathan's street and ducked into an alley when a police car rushed by with red lights blaring. Once the street had cleared, I edged my way out and found my way back to the bus stop. Luckily I had a few coins in my pocket since I left the rest of my belongings in Jonathan's home. I mentally went through what I had in the backpack. Shit. I left my ID. I forced myself to push that to the back of my mind. I needed to stay focused, refocus on Zachary.

I checked my watch and found that I had probably only been there for an hour or so. The adrenaline still alive. I hoped Zach would show up before long. I knew I couldn't leave until he did. Neighbors waved as they passed.

"Waiting for Zach?" one asked.

"Yeah, do you know where he is?"

"Nah. I think he headed out for the night."

Great, I thought. *Just great.* "Thanks," I said. Just as I got up to leave, he came walking down the street with Lena.

"What are you doing here?" he asked. Annoyance clear in his tone.

"I wanted to talk to you," I said.

"Up to more of your bullshit?" Lena asked. She puffed on a cigarette and flicked it into the street. "I'll leave you kids be." She kissed Zach on the cheek. "Shout out if you need me." I watched as she made her way down the street and turned the corner.

The night's stars had been hidden behind smoke from summer brush fires. The air thick with the scent.

"So," I said.

Zach crossed his arms against his chest. "Yes?"

"I'm guessing an apology isn't enough."

"Good guess."

Great. Maybe I should just leave. I stared at him for a moment, trying to figure out what to say and came up with nothing of meaning. Nothing that could take away the last few months. "Okay then." I started down his walkway and as I started to pass him, he stopped me.

"What did you want to say?" he asked.

With those words, I met his gaze. He looked like he searched for something. The same thing I had been searching for and in that moment, I realized I had found it with him. In my head I played out telling him that everything I had done with Jonathan was a mistake. I told him how I was a jerk and a loser and I didn't deserve him. Mentally, I took back every moment I had spent obsessed with someone and I replayed the wonderful moments I had spent with Zach. But instead of telling him these things, these things that I swore he could read in my eyes and he could see in my stance. These were the things he knew the moment he saw me sitting on his front step waiting for him. Instead of saying all of these things, I stepped closer to him and with a breath to his ear, I said, "I'm sorry. I'm ready."

Acknowledgements

The list grows each time I revise the acknowledgements page because there are far too many influencers who impacted the publication of this piece. I will do my best.

Tremendous thanks to my incredible supporters including my editor, Jade Blackwater, my cover art designer, Bookfly Design, the great photographer Chad Alan for my book jacket photo and great images on www.lisadianekastner.com. All of my students/friends/cohorts from the great classes I had the honor to teach. You taught me more than I ever taught you. I am blessed for this.

Huge thanks to Porochista Khakpour, Da Chen, Karen Osborn, Jacquelyn Mitchard, and the rest of the Fairfield University MFA instructors who guided me, nurtured me, and taught me invaluable lessons. Cannot forget my FU MFA brethren who will always be my family including Chris Madden, Sarah Sleeper, Dave DeFusco, Deb Henry, Erin Ollila, Phil Lemos, David LeGere, Ionna Opidee, Brittany Hill, Reuben Hayslett, Daisy Abreu, Susan Smith Daniels, Stephanie Harper, Colin Hosten, A.J. O'Connell, Linsey Jayne, My Clark Kent – Adam Newson, Tommy Hahn, Valerie Lee, Tess Long, Abbey Lopez, and a ton more. I love you all.

Great thanks to those at Yale Writers Conference including Terry Hawkins, MG Lord, Jennifer McCauley, Molly Gaudry, Victoria Rinkerman, Kirsten Bakis, Jotham Burrello, Carol Dowd-Forte, Laura Boswell, Cecile Callan, Scott Jones, Alexandra Marks,

Aimee LaBrie, Srah Haufrect, Alyson Mead, Andrew Adams, Janette Davis, Shreya Dutt, Gaylene Gould, Sue Kochman, David Campbell West, Meg O'Connor, Valorie Ruiz, Breanna Dwyer, Lisa Montagne, Peggy Coe Campbell, Damasa Doyle and so many more. Thank you for letting me into The Tribe.

Bread Loaf Writers' Conference including Aryn Kyle, Alexander Chee, Percival Everett, Danzy Senna. Thank you for your acceptance and guidance.

Squaw Valley Writers Conference where I had the pleasure to hang out with and learn from Kevin Lee and so many others. And a huge thanks to Jamie Ford for tipping me onto the party house. And the biggest thanks to the one conference that is dearest to my heart – Pennwriters Conference. Your community and encouragement will forever lift me up. This is where I first felt at home and where I will always consider my home to be.

Huge thank you to my beta readers including Barbara Lockwood, Jade Blackwater, my dearest husband Bobbie Rae, James Buescher (RIP), Chris Madden, Lizz McCullom.

My thanks to Heather Henderson, Marie Guinto McGuire, Lisa Gillis, Heather Weisband. Thank you for befriending a scared, insecure person. You have no idea how much your friendships meant to me.

Thank you to my family, Frank Earl Kastner, Grace Brenda Kastner, Andrea Kastner, Colin Kastner, Larry Kastner, Marge Kastner, Tom Kastner, Roger Kastner, Lara Kastner, Alexis Kastner, Whitney Kastner, Gene Kastner (RIP), Duncan Kastner, Christy Kastner, Jewel Kastner, Bob Kastner, Megan Davis for being my family.

Thank you to Violet Smith for gifting my first journal that held my thoughts, my fears, my poems, my lyrics. You knew before anyone else what my path would be. Thank you for being one of my biggest advocates. I miss you.

I know I mentioned him once but I need to mention him again – my heart, my soul, my life – Bobbie Rae. Thank you for being my husband, my best friend, my life, my advocate. I am so blessed we are entwined. Looking forward to chasing each other in wheel chairs across the laminated flooring of our retirement home. You best look out – I can build up momentum pretty darn quick.

www.ingramcontent.com/pod-product-compliance
Lightning Source LLC
LaVergne TN
LVHW020711110826
845149LV00012B/2204

* 9 7 8 0 9 9 7 7 7 8 8 0 9 *